# THE COLLECTED CASES OF DUCHESS, PI

LAURA ANNE GILMAN

eBook ISBN 978-0-9894278-6-9
Print ISBN 978-0-9894278-7-6


The cases of Duchess, PI were originally released individually to supporters of Laura Anne Gilman's Patreon. They are collected here for the first time.

# CONTENTS

Dear Reader,

The original "Duchess" was my beloved silver mackerel tabby, Pandora. Both regal and utterly ridiculous, she was my constant companion for over a decade, until a spine injury took her from us.

When I first came up with the idea of writing something to help offset the cost of her "little brother" Boomerang's insulin ($290 per vial, thanks US Big Pharma you greedy bastards), it made perfect sense to me that my Duchess (as she was nick-named) would step forward, offering her name -and her 'tude - to these stories.

I like to think that she - and you, by buying this copy - are still looking after him.

Every bit of *this* Duchess comes from that one. The rest of the crew... well, some of them may still be hanging around. And some may yet to be met.

Enjoy!

Laura Anne
    (and Boomerang and Castiel)

THE CASE OF THE TOM IN TROUBLE

THE FIRST TIME I met the tom, I knew he was going to be trouble. He walked in on a Tuesday afternoon like he owned the place, not an orange tuft out of place, sleek and slick and pretending like he didn't have a problem. I knew he had one; you could see it in his eyes, and anyway, the Human wouldn't send me one who didn't.

That's what I do. I fix problems. They call me the Duchess, and I know every back-alley milk-dealer and fishmonger in the city.

I gestured for him to take a seat, then leaned back on my pillow and blinked at him slowly. "So. What can I do for you?"

Most pusses walk in here, they stammer and stutter and try to pretend they didn't actually come to me for any real reason. He'd clearly been warned I didn't have patience with games, because he coughed it right up.

"It was a few weeks ago. I... I was indiscreet."

Uh-huh. I'd heard the story before; a little too much catnip one night, an invitation to frolic with a clowder he doesn't know, and the next thing he knows there are photos held in unfriendly paws, and an unsigned note: pay up or fess up, to the tune of one grand, cash.

My tail twitched once, but I kept my ears tipped forward, polite as fishes. No matter what you thought of a client, you didn't let them know. Especially not before they'd laid down a retainer, and *never* once they had. But the question had to be asked.

"And you can't say publish and be damned, because...?"

Because his adoption agreement was iron-clad. No midnight wandering, no dead mice on the pillow, and absolutely no nipping around. One wrong move and he'd be out in the alley — or worse, on his way to the vet. Orange tom's whiskers were full and forward-facing, like he'd never smelled anything bad in his lives, but there was a twitch in there that told me he was taking this seriously. Good.

There were a lot of things in this life I didn't like, but I liked blackmailers least of all. Give me an honest fight over skulking and shaming. That didn't mean I was going to be a pushover for the tom, though, no matter how sleek his fur. Pretty boys were always trouble, and I didn't need more trouble in my lives.

I leaned forward, let my claws show. "So, you want me to... what? Haul the blackmailer in for the cops to deal with, or just make those photos go away forever? The latter costs more than the former, and neither's cheap."

The tom's tail twitched, just the tip, like he had everything under control except that quarter-inch of nerves. "I need this dealt with quickly, and quietly."

Of course he did. I make my living off toms like this. If any of them had any sense... well, they didn't, so it wasn't a worry.

"This is my fee," and I pushed a slip of paper across the desk between us. "Retainer plus daily, and a reserve for any bribes I might have to make along the way."

"You're an expensive puss," he said, his whiskers twitching once in dismay.

I groomed my own, letting him know I didn't give a damn what he thought. "You want the best, you pay for the best, pal."

He paid.

* * *

THE TOM'S NAME, it turned out, was Boomerang Took. He wasn't to blame for the name, so I didn't hold it against him. I took his story down again, in detail this time, one step at a time. He'd been down in the tenderloin when the nip incident happened, playing alley cat for kicks.

"I swear, I didn't —"

"Save it," I told him. "I don't care. You're my client now, that makes you pure as fresh-laid litter."

I showed him the door and closed it behind him.

My first call — after depositing his check and making sure it cleared — was to visit the cattery where Mr. Took been rubbing fur that night. I'd heard of it, though I'd never been. It wasn't a high class joint, but the floor was clean and the place didn't have fleas, so that put it above some I'd dipped into.

I went when they'd just opened, before things got busy, and asked to speak with the manager. That got me ushered into his office, a broom closet brooms would find claustrophobic, and the door mostly shut behind us, so the staff could keep a whisker tuned for trouble without overhearing anything that might be bad for them.

The host — a ruffled, tired-eyed tuxedo — gave me a once over, long black tail flicking over the edge of his chair, but he didn't bother with an attempt to shine me on: he knew my type by sight, being good at his job, and was willing to let me do mine. I appreciated that. "What can we do you for?"

"A friend of mine was here, few nights ago. Seems somehow photos were taken?" High class or low, that was a no-no at a nip joint, and the host knew that. His ears flattened, and his tail stilled, green eyes going wide. His distress looked real, but tuxedos were trained for this game: I didn't trust him.

I didn't trust anyone.

"I assure you—"

"Don't want or need assurances, puss. I need to talk to your 'tender," I said. "Someone who worked last Tuesday night." The host might be in charge on paper, but 'tenders were the ones who saw what was going down, whether they were pocketing a percentage or not.

If Tuxedo said no, I was back to square one. I was betting he wouldn't say no: places like this existed on the edge of scary-but-not-dangerous and they couldn't afford to bring the dogs down on them.

"That's be Buster," he said, ears tilting forward. "You're in luck, he's on tonight."

Of course he was. I didn't leave those things to chance. I waited until the host pointed the younger tuxedo out, though; you didn't brush a puss in his own territory.

Buster was leaning on the bar chatting up a young tabby when I came up. The tabby took one look and skedaddled with her tray, her tail held low and still. Buster pushed back, meeting my gaze without twitching a whisker. He was going to be harder to impress.

Good thing I wasn't here to impress him.

I put my card down on the bartop between us, sliding it forward, one claw just barely indenting the paper. "We can do this hard or easy, your call," I said. "But your boss let me in, so I'd advise going easy."

He flicked the dishtowel over one shoulder, looked down at the card, and flicked one ear at me.

"Private eye, huh? And a nice pair of peepers you've got, too," he purred.

"Yes, they are," I agreed. "And they're looking at you. You wanna talk?"

"I get paid to be here no matter what. No tip off my tail how I spend it." His eyes flicked me up and down, then went back to the bowls he'd been cleaning. "What'ya looking to know?"

"There was a tom here last Thursday. Orange boy, standard looker, partying with types he should have walked around. I need the name of his playmates." The idea that the blackmailer is some unknown shadowy figure works better in novels: nine times out of ten, it's someone the victim knows. Someone close-up and personal, who knows where to strike and how hard, for maximum payoff and minimum yowl.

Buster's whiskers twitched, but he kept his ears still. "Mmm, lots of orange boys here, any given night. They like the atmosphere. Can't say's I could pick any one out of the crowd, much less who they cuddled with."

Of course he couldn't. Fortunately, I'd come prepared. My paw slid forward across the bar again, and his claw hooked the bills from underneath, making them disappear fast enough he must sideline as a cop.

Buster must've a simolen-based memory, because the moment he had the cash he was a fount of information. A leaky, cracked fount, but he coughed up a hairball of names. I recognized one of them, a Manx with a pedigree and no first-in-shows.

"You've been a real help, puss."

"Great. So you'll forget you ever came here and I'll do the same." I could see Buster's point: the Manx wasn't much on people spreading her name around.

Buster went back to polishing the milk-bowls, and I found my own way out.

WHEN IN DOUBT, groom. With the check cleared I could have had my choice of salons but I'm a loyalist and I went to Fifi's.

There was an aging calico in the chair when I got there, and I was careful not to let my eyes rest on her longer than it took for us to both acknowledge each other, avoiding even the hint of a challenge. Queens are cranky by nature and aging queens crankier than most, and everyone knows calicos are batshit crazy. The combination wasn't something I wanted to rile, even though Fifi would've knocked both of us flat on our tails if either one of us had started a hiss.

Fifi's receptionist Dot came through the curtain separating the back rooms from the front, settling behind the delicate writing desk that passed as their reception area before noticing I'd come in. "Duchess, doll! It's been ages!"

She practically quivered, restraining the urge to get up and hug me. I let my tail twine with hers as I passed — she was a good kit, Dot was, even if she had the manners of a Pomeranian sometimes.

"You know how it is," I said, swiping a saucer and pouring myself a dash of the tar Fifi claims is coffee. Her theory is, it'll kill us sooner rather than later, why not enjoy the ride?

There are reasons I go to Fifi's, and her touch with the trimmers is only part of it.

The Calico queen finished up and waddled over to the dryers, and I slipped into the hot-seat. Fifi barely looked up, wiping down the table and resetting her tools in a workmanlike fashion. Nobody knew how old Fifi was; the torn ear and limp in her hindquarters could have come from a fight two years back or twenty, and her silver-grey fur wasn't telling any secrets. Her green eyes were still clear, and her paws steady as she picked up my left paw and pushed, extending the claws so she could decide what needed to be done.

"Hmmm. You've been scratching again, and not in good places."

"You always scold, and I never change." She'd told me to buy a good-quality sisal for the office and use it at least twice a week, but with my hours, well... sometimes you gotta take what's available when it's available. But she didn't want to hear why I'd gone *garra a garra* with a cement wall last month. My cuticles still hadn't recovered, as she was now well-aware.

"Tsk." She plunged all four paws into a warm bath of god-knows-what, and pushed back her roller-chair, whiskers pulled back in a disapproving scowl. That was why I'd avoided stopping by earlier; once she had you in the hot seat, there was no getting out — or away. "Not that you ever listen to my advice —"

"Fifi, I *come here* for your advice," I responded, and it was mostly the truth. I didn't ask for it, but when she gave it, I listened. And she always gave it.

"Hrmph. I told you to carry a nail file with you, too, keep your edges trimmed, but do you listen to that?"

"Yes." I carried it with me at all times. I wasn't going to mention that the last time I'd used it had been to pick a lock, though. That reminded me, I needed to replace it.

"Then you need lessons in how to use it," she said, but her whiskers loosened a little, and her eyes softened. Fifi was a tough old broad — she had to be, with a dog's name — but she also saw herself as litter-mother to all us working dolls. "Upsadaisy," and she tapped my left front paw, wiping it expertly with a towel and then pressing the pad again until my claws were spread for her to get at. "Anything fancy today?"

"Just the usual, please," even as she was already reaching for the clear gloss. Fancy kept pusses might opt for colors or sparkles, but in my job, you didn't want to flash any glam you couldn't drop, and you never wanted anything the cops might be able to scrape off and pin on you later. And colored gloss was definitely in the latter category.

"So, what brings you here now, after so long away, if it's not to finally add some life to your colors?"

"My colors are just fine, Fifi." I didn't bother curbing my words: with the Calico under the dryers, it was just me and Fifi and Dot here now, and Dot wouldn't say a word Fifi had't told her to, and Fifi wouldn't say so unless I told her to. "But I may be walking with some upper-window types for this job, and you'll make sure I don't put myself to shame."

"Mmmmm. How upper-window?"

"Penthouse." Not entirely, not unless I'd misread Orange Tom completely, which I never did. But better to aim high and have them assume you're slumming than aim too low and be tossed out into the alley. "And you get more with cream than you do skim."

"Hmmmm." Fifi evened up the claws on one paw with terrifying speed, then moved on to the other. "You looking to rub up against city folk, you're going to need more than a polish and a trim if something goes wrong."

Again, she didn't say, but her whispers were disapproving.

"Already covered," I reassured her, then leaned back and let her take care of the hind paws as well. Sometimes, a girl's just got to relax and enjoy the massage chair, right?

---

THERE'S nothing like newly-shaped and lacquered claws to make a puss feel invincible. Fifi was an artist: I couldn't even feel the polish against my sheaths, but when I stretched a claw, there it was, glinting back at me, a quiet and secret pleasure. And I was going to need all the secret quiet pleasures I could get, because my next stop was to take care of the thing I'd promised Fifi I'd taken care of already.

And that meant braving the dog's den.

I paused outside of the station, staring up at the red shingles, and sighed. Not that every member of the force was a dog, but even the ones who weren't had a certain pack mentality that made my ears go flat on instinct.

There was a Cocker pup at the front desk, shuffling paper like it was his last hope of salvation. I leaned against the counter and gave him my best 'harmless but useful' look. "I'm here to see Lieutenant Sparks."

Cocker didn't look impressed. "You got an appointment?"

"Yes."

That pinned his ears back in surprise, and he took a closer look at me, like I was yanking his collar.

"Really," I said, stretching out one paw idly, letting the overhead fluorescents catch on the diamond-edged tip. "Do be a darling, sergeant, and fetch him, will you?"

He snarled, one edge of his drooping lip pulled back in silent disapproval, but he jammed the call button and told the good captain that I was out there waiting.

It only took a few minutes for Sparks to have me buzzed back into the sanctum, despite the fact that I didn't in fact have an appointment.

It was a miserable little sanctum, as things go: dreary green walls and a few wilted potted plants, but the floor underneath wasn't cracked, and the air hummed through well enough to filter out the smells the rest of the building was heir to, courtesy of the holding cells downstairs and the general state of misery this place carried on its back.

"What is it this time?"

Sparks never wasted time on pleasantries: it was part of why we got along. Although 'got along' would overstate the fact considerably. Better to say that we had a grudging respect for each others' competence. It was enough.

"I'm not here to ask a favor," I assured him, not bothering to take a seat: I wouldn't scrape my nails on that sofa, much less place my body on it. "I just wanted to give you an ears-up."

Sharp white teeth flashed in what nobody sane would consider a smile. "Me personally, oh joy. What did I do to earn this honor?" Sparks was a Shepherd crossbreed: sarcasm came natural with the genetics.

"I have a client who got himself into a bit of a tangle with the sorts he shouldn't. And I'm going to untangle him, but there may be fallout in the next day or so. Of the sort you might be able to turn into a biscuit or two tossed your way by Uptown."

We all might walk the independent walk, but nobody says no to scritches. Especially if they might come with a promotion. Sparks was ambitious, to go with decent looks and adequate smarts, and some day he'd make Captain, which would be useful to both of us.

"And I'll know this fallout when it lands on my nose?" He wasn't scoffing, though, and he wasn't demanding I give him details I wasn't at liberty to give. And that was why he got the freebie: he might be a dog, but he knew when not to dig.

"I'll let you know, if you miss it," I promised, and turned to leave.

"Hey, Duchess."

I paused, ears twitching, but didn't turn around again.

"Am I gunna owe you for this?"

It was tempting: an open-ended favor could come in handy. But so would his knowing I *could* have said yes and didn't.

"Call it a once-a-lifetime freebie," I said instead, and took that as my exit cue.

MY NEXT STOP was checking out the Manx Buster'd spilled on. That address took me to a strip of the City about as upwind as you could get, where the houses not only had doors, they had doormen.

Our respectable citizens lift their noses when they talk about the alley, the gutter-hunters and the lost, but the smell of urine and musk aren't the worst things in the world. First thing a smart kit learns is that the City's like an onion, and not just 'cause it'll all end in tears. There are layers, and you gotta be careful when you peel 'm back. Also, you leave things long enough, there's gonna be rot.

I scratched at the door, and waited while they checked my bona fides, and then checked to see if the mistress of the house would deign to see me.

Much to the butler's surprise, she would.

The stink of money and ennui filled the room I'd been ushered into, and it made me want to sneeze. Or maybe those were the lilies falling out of vases everywhere. The Manx was curled on a pillow that probably cost more than I'd make in a month, the nubby black fabric showing her creamy blue fur to perfection.

"The...Duchess, ma'am. Will there be anything else?" I'd never have tapped a terrier for butler, but the little rat did obsequious like he'd been born to it.

"Excellent," the Manx purred. "That will be all," and she waved a paw in dismissal. The butler flicked his tail once, clearly unhappy, then closed the door behind me, leaving the two of us alone together.

The Manx was rounded and soft, but I didn't make the mistake of thinking that made her stupid. She had let me in because she was bored. If I didn't entertain her, I'd be out on my ear before my whiskers could twitch.

"You're new. I like new."

"I bet you do, sister." I'm not much for swagger, but any puss with hips and a tail can knock it out if they try. "Your boy gave you my card, so you don't have to pretend you don't know who I am." It's not that I think I've got a rep big enough for the city to know about me, but if the Manx was playing with alley cats, odds were, she knew about me.

"And what could a tough private eye want with little ole' me?" Her lids closed lazily, but those dark blue eyes were watching me from underneath like I was a mouse she planned to have served up for dinner.

"I'd say the pleasure of your company, but that would only be half true. I'm a blunt puss, sister, I don't know how else to be. You might know something, have seen something, that could help me out. So I'm here to find out if you do in fact know it."

No mention of the tom, since I didn't know how they'd parted ways. Keep her focused on me, intrigue her, smooth her fur a little to think I needed her, that something of the alley might involve her. That's what bored, well-bred cats like her did; dangle a claw in the rough, without getting any on her perfectly-curled whiskers. She might have been raised on salmon and cream, but even that could get boring, too. Or so I'd been told.

"And why would I want to help you out?"

She was playing it cool, and her lack of a tail might have meant some others couldn't read her, but there was a tremor in that silky topcoat, and her claws peeked out just enough to rasp at the surface of her pillow. I let my ears flick forward, my tail curl over the edge of my own pillow, the tip twitching just enough to catch her attention, but not enough to distract her from what I was saying. "Because it'd be fun."

I'd been dead-on. Gorgeous — that was her name, it turned out, and it suited her down to her dewclaw — was as bored as she was beautiful, and I was the answer to her afternoon prayer. And I'd been right about the cream and salmon. By the time I strolled out of her den, I was purring from more than a job well-done, my tummy tight with too many scraps. If anyone'd taken that moment to pay back old debts I'd've been in trouble, but fortunately, I wasn't on anyone's agenda that afternoon.

She'd been there the night in question, Gorgeous had, and remembered the tom with detailed appreciation. She also remembered the bit of rough he'd rubbed against, and the rough's companion, who had taken offense at what Gorgeous said had just been a crowded dance floor incident, no harm intended.

"So, there was a fight?"

"Nothing so interesting. Security stepped in before they moved past hissing and growling." She'd been disappointed.

"Tell me about the companion."

"Nothing special." Her rounded shoulders lifted in a shrug, her paw reaching out to scoop up another bit of salmon from the plate, licking it delicately from between two claws. "Creamiscle white belly, head like a rock. The pick of a liter you don't mind if someone drowns."

That was all I needed to hear. I'd thanked her for her cooperation, and hot-pawed it back outside, not stopping until I was on more familiar streets. I could still scent the stink of those flowers on my fur, and paused to groom myself back into shape, rid myself of the stink while I thought about what to do next.

The fact that the tom hadn't mentioned that didn't surprise me. Either he, typical male, hadn't thought a shoulder-bump was important, or he'd known it was important but had also thought it was embarrassing. Embarrassment seems to up the dumb factor in everyone and forgetting to mention that he'd accidentally — or not — put paws on Dumpster's current puss was absolutely dumb.

Some of the alley-dwellers aren't bad sorts, they ended up there through bad luck or worse lives and made the best of it they could. Then there were the ones like Dumpster. Dig a little and you had a nice suburban cat named Peaches McCream. With a name like that, it wasn't hard to see why he'd rather sleep on concrete than a cushy bed, but Dumpster went too far; he got out on the street and went bad. Not just a roughneck or a bully; Dumpster liked seeing others go down, too.

And it sounded like maybe he'd decided Boomerang Took was the next to take down.

I finished sorting of my fur, and lowered my leg, still thinking. I knew of Dumpster, but I was pretty sure he didn't know me by sight. I'd kept it that way intentionally. But all good things come to an end, eventually. Gorgeous had been as helpful as she could — and hinted that she'd like to be more helpful, so long as it didn't involve her actually getting mud on her paws — but if this was the way the scent led, I was going to need more experienced help. And maybe then I'd be able to cause the fallout I'd promised Captain Sparks, as well as clear my client.

Ideally, without getting any mud on my own paws, too.

"My next life, I'm coming back as a house cat," I told the spider dangling from the awning. The spider, only having the one life to worry about, ignored me.


WHEN YOU NEED help of the sort I needed, there's only one place you go. Momma's.

The sentry on the stoop was napping, but both eyes were open by the time I came within reach. "Long time no see, Princess."

"Bite me, Squeak." I bopped him on the nose as I passed. Squeak had gotten tossed from a moving car when he was a kitten; his hind legs didn't work and that should've been the end of him then and there. Except then and there was when Momma was strolling past.

Far as I could tell, Momma hadn't ever had a litter of her own, owing to a stint at the local shelter when she was young. But that hadn't stopped her: at any given time there were a dozen or more kitlings scrambling around, and a handful more of her olders, who'd decided to stick around and join the family business. Squeak had been one of those, and for all that he rarely moved from his spot at the door, he had his paw on the pulse of nearly everything that went down in Alleytown.

And what he didn't know, one of the others would find out. That was half of the family business: knowing things.

The other half was hunting them.

"Momma." I let her groom my ears in welcome, even though I knew there hadn't been a hair out of place. "I need to borrow Sammy."

The grooming paused, then she put a paw on my head and pushed down and away, indicating that she was done. I slunk back a pace, and settled myself on my haunches.

"Sammy!"

A lean, lithe tiger leaped over a clowder and stalked over to join us. Sammy's eyes were bright with interest, and his whiskers pulled back so tight they practically quivered. His ears were intact, his coat unscarred, but he was the best rough-and-tumbler Momma had to offer.

"Duchess wants to borrow you for a bit. You interested?"

It wasn't really a question; if Momma hadn't wanted him to go, she wouldn't have called him over.

"We going clean, or dirty?"

"Dirty all the way," I told him.

"Then I'm in."

I UNLOCKED the office door and ushered Sammy in. He immediately homed in on the low-slung cushion under the window, then immediately abandoned it to prowl around the space, sniffing. "Nice digs."

"Don't get too comfortable; we're not staying."

I didn't like bringing any of Momma's brood to my office, but I needed to check messages, and send a few, before we headed out again. Second thing you learn about doing something incredibly stupid: make sure people know where you're going and who you're meeting with, in case anything goes bad. The one to the Human went direct, the one to the captain was on a delivery delay, and gave more detail: if I'd gone down a life, he'd need to know who to bite, and how hard.

And if I came back in one piece, he'd never know I'd asked him to do anything. Better for our relationship, that way.

"Hey!" I hissed at Sammy when he tried poking his whiskers into the file cabinet. "You want to waste a life that easy?"

I waited until he settled himself back on the cushion, exuding an air of wounded innocence that would have been laughable if it weren't so convincing. Momma trains them, but Sammy had a natural aptitude. If he'd chosen to go into politics rather than crime, he could have been dangerous.

"So, what've you tagged me for, anyway?"

"I need you to break me in somewhere."

"Cream. Where?"

"Dumpster's den."

I'd give the kit credit, all the response that got was a twitch of an ear, and the slow widening of his eyes. "When you go crazy you don't go crazy small, do you."

"You want out?"

"Oh hell no. I'd trade two lives to be able to be known as the puss who bit Dumpster's tail."

And that was why I hated using amateurs, even talented ones. "It'll be worth *all* of your lives if anyone finds out."

That got another ear twitch, and a sigh. "That sucks." Then the eternal optimism of youth kicked back in. "But I'll know. And he'll know someone bit him, right?"

"Right." I had no idea, actually. But it was easier to let him be enthusiastic about keeping a secret than worrying that he'd yowl it to the moon. "You bring your tools?"

That quiet glee turned to scornful superiority. "Of course." A flick of his claws, and I could see where the keratin had been modified, half of them tipped in metal, the other half cut or gouged into specialized shapes.

"You better hope the barkers never catch you," I said, and got another scornful look.

"I cap 'em when I'm not working."

"Cap 'em now," I told him, and waited while he did, his tail lashing in a sulk all the while.

I closed down the laptop and locked it on the file cabinet, SOP when I wasn't sure if I'd be coming back soon, and smoothed down my fur, the only sign of nerves I allowed myself. "Let's go."

"We're doing it now? In daylight?"

Save me from amateurs.

---

"So, what are we looking for?"

"We're not looking for anything. You're getting me inside and keeping watch. I'm looking."

"You don't trust me,"

I haven't perfected the burn-to-ash-with-a-look yet. But I keep trying.

Dumpster's den was nicer than he had any right to, considering his name and his personal grooming habits. It was a pretty little mid-Century split-level, with a rock garden that probably required more upkeep than a lawn, and bay windows that could fit half a dozen sunbeam nappers, at a pinch. I mean, I'm more of a modernist, but this looked cozy enough to make Martha Stewart hack a hairball in envy. We were half a block away, to all appearances grabbing a patch of sunlight on a fence, as one does. Worst thing you can do when casing a joint is look like you're casing a joint.

Sammy had picked up a snack on the way up and was cleaning feathers out of his claw. "Okay, I get it, I'm just the hired help. Don't tell me anything. No idea who's in the house, or how many, or the layout, or what kind of a system they've got other than expensive."

"If it were easy it'd've been done already."

"Right. Back left side window, second floor. Give me.... Seven, then follow."

You get used to waiting, in this gig. Waiting for something to happen, waiting for someone to tell you the truth, waiting to get paid... I'd like to think it gets easier at some point, but I haven't gotten there yet. I let my tail droop over the back of the fence, practically taunting the crows in the tree behind me to grab it. They called back the usual rude taunt and, formalities exchanged, we went back to ignoring each other. Four... Five... at six, I leapt down from the fence, landing on the single patch of dry ground in the garden, picking my way through whatever greenery the residents had planted. I could identify common flowers in a bouquet, but that was about it. They smelled good, though, green and bright, and the bees and bugs had a contented, happy sound to their chatter.

A good life, if a short one. I wondered if bees had blackmail, bribery, murder, theft... well, theft they knew, I guess, if they lived in a hive. Bears or humans, eventually someone was gonna get ya.

At the count of seven, I dropped off the fence and padded my way to the left side of the house, looking up at the second floor. There was a flutter of the curtains, then the glass slid up, just enough for me to fit my head through.

That was enough. I made my way up the nearest tree, worked my way along the branch, and judged the distance between me and the window ledge, then jumped.

Fortune may favor the brave, but calculus and physics help even the odds. My claws scraped along the gutter, but I'd landed at the right angle, and was able to squeeze my head under the ledge, the rest of my body following.

Inside, Sammy was waiting, his tail curled around his haunches and his whiskers totally pleased with himself. I took a look around the room: there were four beds, the circular kind you could pick up in any supply store, nothing special, and the smell of a litter box coming from the half-open closet. Under that, I could pick up the scent of at least five different toms, so this room wasn't saved for anyone special, probably where his henchpaws of the week stayed, when they had guard duty.

It stank like testosterone and herring.

"There are three down the hallway, and two downstairs" Sammy said quietly, his ego thankfully not shredding the common sense his Momma taught him. "They're sober but lazy; did one patrol down the hallway but didn't look up or check any closed doors."

"Dumpster?"

"Not here." I could hear the disappointment in his voice. It was one thing to break into Dumpster's home base, but to do it when the puss himself was in residence? I twitched an ear at him and headed for the door. Let the young and dumb wish for glory; I'd be grabbing what I came for and — hopefully — be gone without anyone ever knowing we were there.

"Did you happen to find his —"

"Office? Two doors down." He flicked a single claw, showing off. "I unlocked it for you."

"Good work, kid." It's not ego-stroking when they actually earn it. I poked my whiskers into the hallway and, when they told me it was clear, headed for the second door on the left, across the hall. I wasn't a mind-reader: it was the only one with an obviously enhanced lock under the door latch. Dumpster wasn't dumb: he didn't trust his own people any more than he trusted other people.

The office was nothing more or less than I'd expected from Dumpster: the desk was mahogany, the walls were covered in sissal, the floor carpeted in plush thicker than my client's fur — not that I'd had a chance to check the actual depth of it — and, when I took a check into the closet, sure enough the damned litter box was at very least *plated* in gold.

"Dumpster, you pretentious bastard," I said to the empty air. "You probably think your scat smells like fresh mouse, too."

I went back to the desk, studying it. Too large, too obvious, with its scratcher-pad and feather quill pen, like he wrote his correspondence out rather than sending a thug to break some paws when he wanted to send a message.

"Whatever you're looking for can you get a move on?" Sammy had positioned himself by the window, occasionally taking a glance through the curtains, careful not to disturb them. "Just cause the house is quiet don't mean it'll stay that way all day."

Dumpster wouldn't put anything important in this desk. He was arrogant, but he was also paranoid. Where...

The gold-plated litter box lingered in my thoughts. He wouldn't...

He might.

He had.

"You flea-bitten bastard," I muttered, after lifting the box and shifting it to the side to reveal the lockbox set in the floor underneath. "I suppose I should be thankful you didn't make me scratch through your scat for it, too."

The lockbox wasn't locked: he was paranoid, but not so much that he considered anyone being as clever as him a real risk. Inside, there were an even dozen packets, each with a name on them.

I was tempted to take them all, but that wasn't what I was being paid for. I did make note of each name, though. I couldn't do anything with them, but the barkers might be able to poke around, maybe scratch out enough dirt to give Sparks some of what he needed to make Captain. Step three: profit.

I tucked the folder away and turned to my companion. "Out the way we came in?"

Sammy grinned at me. "Always."

Only problem was, the window was closed. And we weren't alone.

---

"Aw, Duchess. If you'd wanted to come for a visit, you shoulda called."

If my client had been a bit too sleek, Dex made up for it on the other side of the scale. His grey and white fur matted around his ruff, and his ears were notched like a bedpost from the fights he'd been in. But under the fur and the scars there was sold muscle, and the muscle between his ears was nothing to sneer at either.

I knew all that firsthand.

"You'd just sulk because I wasn't here to see you." Just because we'd parted on reasonably good terms didn't mean he was going to be a pushover for my charms, such as they were. I settled down on my haunches, made sure my ears were erect, despite every instinct to flatten them against my skull, and stilled the tip of my tail, tucking it demurely under my paws. The envelope I'd taken was tucked under my tummy, and not for the first time I wished for longer fur, the better for hiding things in. Sammy sidled up next to me, his head low and his body tucked against the floor, by all first-glances a kitten in the presence of adults. But I felt him nudge against me, his body covering whatever of the envelope might have peeked out, and the instinct to groom the tip of his ears in approval was strong.

I refrained, though; there was no need to give Dex anything he could possibly use.

"You here to ask the boss for a job? Well, the boss ain't here, though I know he'll be sorry to have missed you..." Dex was watching us both, eyes slitted and pupils dilated. He knew full-well I wasn't here to lick Dumpster's ears in hopes of a handout.

"You know me, Dex. I like my independence, even if it doesn't come with milk and a collar."

That got a coughed laugh from him, and I remembered why we'd tried to make a go of it once; he had a sense of humor, even if he couldn't keep his tail down. "Milk, collar, and a steady wrapper of fish, Duchess. Now come on, why're you here? I can't believe you'd slum so low as to be twining tails with any of these mooks, so don't break my heart and tell me it's so."

A sense of humor, and a possessive streak. I hadn't forgotten about that.

"Come on, puss. Whatcha here for? And why dincha use the front door like a friend?"

I'd have one chance to get us out of here without trouble. I had to make it believable. Something brazen enough for him to respect, but smart enough for him to believe.

"It's him," and I dropped my chin to rest it on Sammy's lowered head. "Kitten's got it into his whiskers that he's the best ever sneaker and breaker in town, for all that he's barely grown into his fur. So I thought I'd give him a real challenge." I let out a huff of laughter that carried honest amusement — the only way to convince him I wasn't whistling. "And damned if he isn't nearly as good as he thinks he is. Either that, or your security's got serious problems you should be looking at."

All seven claws stilled: I'd diverted his attention. "You, kid? You're the one that slipped the back door?"

I could feel Sammy's tail twitch; he wasn't happy he'd left enough trace on the door to be found. But that was in character, it helped sell the story. "Yeah." I felt him gather himself, hoped he wasn't going to do anything stupid I couldn't drag him out of. In a fair fight, we'd be dead in minutes, and I didn't think this would be a fair fight. "You got pretty good security, but I'm better."

Dex flexed his toes, showing off his extra claw sheaths, which was about as subtle as Dex got. 'Dactyls were bastards in a claw fight; the two extra claws gave them a mean advantage. "Careful who you say that to, kitten. Could get you gutted for strings, the wrong person hears you."

"Could get me a cushy gig, the right person hears *about* me," Sammy retorted. Good kid. Idiot, but a good kid; either by luck or chance he'd said exactly the right thing.

Hell, for all I knew, this was exactly what he'd hoped would happen. I'd hate to think he'd sell me out like that, didn't think Momma would be happy with him if he did, but it's every puss for themselves, on the street. I knew that, and I respected it.

Dex dismissed Sammy, his gaze focused back on me. "Tell me true, Duchess; you here for any other reason?"

I hated lying to Dex. Not because I had anything against lying, as such, or lying to Dex in particular, but the more times you tell them the truth, the easier they swallow the lie when it comes.

"Swear it on my eighth life," I said, staring him straight in the eye, not a whisker twitching. "Figured the kit here would piss himself the moment he figured out where I'd taken him, maybe fumble the lock and get his ass kicked. Didn't think he'd actually pull it off."

"Hey." Sammy twitched, every inch the indignant, insulted tom, his tail lashing out and knocking over a vase that had been standing innocently by the wall. I started, but Dex moved every bit as fast as I remembered, catching the vase before it was halfway tipped. He moved it back into place, then turned to stare at Sammy.

"You want some advice, squirt, you need more than fast claws to make it in this gig."

"Yessir."

I'd taken advantage of Dex's distraction to shift the folder out of sight. If we got out of here intact, and I didn't kill him the moment we were outside, Sammy might make a decent sneak some day. If he could keep his mouth shut, anyway.

"But I got the fast claws," Sammy went on, flicking his ears forward. "I can learn everything else."

Old Deuteronomy on a popsicle stick. I downvised my estimate of Sammy's chances, and started walking casually toward the door like we had run of the place. "Sammy, with me, and no back-hiss. Dex, you know the kid can do it. Don't tell your boss about Sammy here for at least a year. Let the idiot grow some whiskers, first. Then you can claim credit for finding him."

"It's like you know me, Duchess." Dex watched us go like he knew something was up but couldn't sniff out quite what it was. "But I gotta file a report on this little incursion of yours, or someone's gonna file it for me, if you know what I mean."

The mooks he'd mentioned earlier. He might be Dumpster's captain, but the troops were about as loyal as rats.

"Yeah. I get you. But you don't gotta file it right away, do you?"

He knew something was up. But he didn't know what, and Dex took care of himself, first. He let me go, I owed him, above and beyond Sammy's finder's fee. And we both knew it.

"Sammy. Now."

Sammy followed me down the hallway, ears still forward, tail upright, but the tip twitched like he was trying to scent the air with it.

"Chill," I told him. "You wanted to play, this is how it's played. Right into the dog's mouth, like you already pulled his teeth." I nodded regally to one of the mooks who appeared in a doorway, and kept moving, down the stairs, past headless sculptures in alcoves that had to be a Human's idea of a joke.

We'd just made it past the front door, when three more mooks appeared, two of them with brass claws already pulled over their paws. Alley brawlers gone pro. We weren't going to talk our way past them.

"Dog grew more teeth," Sammy said, just as the mooks closed in.


I woke up feeling like a rat had died in my mouth and I'd forgotten to chew it. I was on the floor — a cold, hard floor, and the lights were too bright. And the file I'd been holding was gone.

"Duchess?"

Sammy, his voice high-pitched as a kitten's.

"Yeah kid, I'm here. Where's here?" I opened my eyes a little more, letting my pupils adjust to the overload. White everywhere: hard plastic walls and floor, deeply unsanitary facilities set in the far corner.

"They put us in a *kennel?*"

Sammy huddled further into his corner at my growl.

"Well now, you wouldn't expect me to set you up in the best guest room, would you?"

A shadow moved just beyond the bars of the door, coming up close enough for me to count his whiskers — but not, sadly, close enough to pull any of them. I'd never meet the puss in person, but there was only one puss it could be, with that splotch of cream and orange over his face. Dex's boss, the one and only Dumpster.

My ears went flat, and my tail lashed before I could control it.

"Duchess, right? I've heard about you." He tapped the file in his paw as though my name was written in there somewhere.

"Only bad things, I'm sure." Ears *up*, I told them. They didn't listen.

Dumpster chuckled, still tapping that file with a nail, the noise like a bark on my nerves. "I suppose that depends on your point of view."

"My point of view is that I have a splitting headache, I'm locked in a kennel, and since you're holding that file, you have no intention of either getting me a painkiller or letting us go." Blackmailers were slimy, but they were simple slime. Dumpster had something more going on, to have us locked up here.

"Oh, you must think me a terrible host." He moved away from the gate, speaking over his shoulder. "Brutus, get the lady a painkiller."

Brutus had been named by someone with a sense of humor: no Maltese had ever managed to look like a Brutus in the history of the bred. But he worked for Dumpster, so I wasn't going to make dumb assumptions.

A packet of nip slipped through the bars of the kennel door. I sniffed at it but didn't pick it up.

"It's perfectly safe," Dumpster said, bored with my hesitation. "If I wanted to drug you, I'd take the more enjoyable route, rather than letting you ingest it unaware."

I extended a claw and pulled the packet toward me. The familiar, calming scent of Valerian floated through the paper. I sighed, and let my chin rest on the packet, allowing the herbs to do their work.

Sammy, having decided that we probably weren't going to die right away, and proving he was half as smart as he thought he was, curled up in the corner, tail over his toes, and watched the two of us with cautious eyes.

Dumpster waited until the painkiller kicked in, then stepped forward, a claw tapping against the side of our kennel. "I'll only ask once. Who sent you?"

He'd need more nip than that to get me to sing for him. But there was no need giving him ideas. Play the dumb puss, and see what he spilled, first. "You're asking me to reveal a client?"

"I'm asking you to be the smart puss your rep says you are. Nobody's gonna know 'cept you and me."

"And everyone else in this room." Plus my client, when whatever was going down fell on him.

"Brutus doesn't talk. And I'm sure you can keep your kitten quiet."

"Not my kit," I said, projecting utter don't-give-a-toot. "He's Momma's."

"That's your worry, not mine. Who. Sent. You."

I thought about the folders in that box. Thought about the

names on those folders, how many of them there were. I'm just a simple PI: I do the job they pay me to do, and I don't spend much time wondering why, or what it all means. But I had a reasonably good grasp on the big picture, too. You have to, if you're gonna survive.

"Tell me why you gotta know, and I'll tell you who."

Those pale green eyes of Dumpster's slitted, and I could practically seem him resist the urge to groom his whiskers like a movie villain, about to spill his evil plan. That's the thing about cats like him: they know they're smart, but they need other people to know it, too.

"My own curiosity," I added. "If I'm gonna sell out a client, I want to know why."

"Curiosity, Duchess. You know what they say about that."

Yeah, I knew. "Do we have a deal? Or are you gonna start pulling claws and breaking tails?"

If he were going to go that route, he would have already. And someone who *deserved* the name Brutus would be in here with us, instead.

"The young fellow in this folder is, in and of himself, utterly useless. Another pet," and Dumpster managed to put three syllables of sneer into that word, "thinking the world's his for the asking. But he's found himself a comfortable bed to sleep in, and his desire to not lose it makes him profitable."

"Money? I'd hoped for something a little more original from you, Dumpster."

"Not money, little tabby. Power. One compromised pet here, another there... soon enough, I'll have the cat-door keys to the entire city in my paw. I'll know what's going to happen, and when, before anyone else. Anyone can get their claws on money. But knowledge? That's how you become king."

The faintest hiss came from Sammy, who clamped his paw over his nose when he realized it. Momma's boy, through and through, and she would not like the thought of anyone else having more information than she could lay claw on.

"So why do you even need to know who my client is?" If Boomerang Took wasn't important enough for someone else to protect him, it was obvious who my client had to be.

"I don't," Dumpster admitted. "I was curious to know what your price would be, to break. You were cheaper than I thought, Duchess. I'm disappointed."

"Terribly sorry about that." I really wasn't. I was also sure he hadn't told me even close to the truth. "So, what now?"

"Now? I put this folder back where it belongs, and you consider your sins, while I consider what to do with you."

"Uh-huh. And him?" I jerked a dewclaw at Sammy.

Dumpster gave the kit a once-over. "He's Momma's, I'll let Momma decide."

Sammy may have whimpered a little at that. I didn't really blame him. Momma's first law was thou shalt not get caught. And there was only so much he'd be able to blame on me.

Not that it mattered. Dumpster'd gotten ambitious, and ambitions didn't like leaving loose ends.

---

Dumpster left us in the kennel to stew, closing the external door with the soft snick that told me it locked automatically. Sammy hadn't uncurled himself, although his tail had flicked more comfortably around his hindquarters, and his eyes were open a slit, watching me.

I had no idea what he saw, and wasn't really curious about it, either. If I didn't get Sammy back to Momma in one, maybe two pieces, she'd be annoyed with me, but she'd be more annoyed with him. So his job was to follow my lead, not give me any whisker, and not do anything stupid. More stupid than we'd already done, anyway. My mood soured: the catnip had obviously worn off, although my headache hadn't returned. Yet.

Dumpster was lying. He'd wanted to know who'd hired me. No, he'd wanted to know who my client was. That was a distinction with a difference, maybe. My thoughts scrambled, trying to resort all the pieces in my head. Just because I'd never gotten played before didn't mean I couldn't be. Was Boomerang Took really a dumb but innocent victim? Or was he playing his own game?

The Human had warned me once, long ago, that no matter how cynical you got, you couldn't ever keep up.

"Ah, fleas." If Took had played me, there wasn't anything I could do about it now. Step one, get out of here. Step two, I'd worry about once we got out of here.

"He's going to kill us. He's going to kill us and skin us and sell us for parts in the market. Maybe not in that order."

"If he doesn't, I will, if you don't shut up," I snapped. I'd never had a litter, but queen-voice seems to be coded into us anyway: Sammy dropped his chin to the floor and shut up.

With quiet came... well, quiet. My earls flicked forward, trying to catch some sound from what I knew should be a busy house above us, but there was nothing, not so much as a scritch of a claw or the creak of a door. Either he'd moved us somewhere else — unlikely, considering how long we'd been out, and how arrogant Dumpster was — or the room was tighter'n a mouse's unmentionables.

That went with the self-locking doors.

The kennel's walls didn't show any bloodstains, and there weren't any drains in the floor. That was some comfort, but not enough. There are ways to get information out of people that don't break the skin or leave an external mess.

Was Dumpster really going to just leave us here, or would he come back, this time less friendly?

The PI business is about sniffing out pieces and putting them together. What did I know for a fact, so far? Dumpster had branched out from petty thug to blackmailer. Why? Not for the money, but power.

I poked at that with my claws. A cat may look at a king, but anyone with sense knows it's better for the king to look to the cat. Kings have the best kitchens. But a wise king knows who's in those kitchens. Maybe it wasn't Took who'd been playing me, but his king? That could be what Dumpster was trying to find out — if his prey had become the predator?

If so, it might be that Took's only sin had been sleeping in a too-soft bed. Well, that and being an idiot, but more cats fell into that than not, I'd found. Especially the sleek ones.

I don't know why that made me feel better, but it did. Even though the end result was going to be the same, if I couldn't get out of here before Dumpster came back — or we died of boredom.

I looked sideways at Sammy, who was grooming between his claws, the picture of casual indifference if you didn't notice the way the tip of his tail kept twitching, like a furred metronome. It was bad enough I could feel my own tail trying to match it and scowled at him before looking back at the walls.

Having determined that there was nothing in our kennel other than depressing kennel-ness, I switched my attention to the door of our kennel. It hinged on the outside, because all nine of my lives hated me like that, but there was a deadbolt on the other side that someone with long, slender claws might be able to dislodge.

I looked down at mine, and my whiskers twitched. I'd dressed for the wrong party.

"Sammy. Get over here."

By the time the tiger slipped under my shoulder to look at

the door, he'd figured out what I was looking at, and what I wanted him to do.

"Possible?"

"Maybe," he said, dubiously.

"Try."

They'd taken his tools, naturally, but he was young enough that his claws were still flexible, and he left them naturally long.

"Come on, baby," he muttered, scrunching up to the door, the side of his face pressed against the white plastic, black nose touching the narrow crack between door and wall. I kept an anxious eye through the bars, anticipating the slightest change in sound, or light, or the door outside opening and someone coming in. "Come on, come on..."

There was a faint, dull metallic click, then Sammy swore as it scraped off his nail, and fell back into place. "You scruffy excuse for a nerf-herding..."

I tuned him out, whiskers quivering as something in the room outside our kennel changed. But the door to the outside hadn't opened, I was certain of that. And the smell...

"Loki."

"What?" Sammy yelped, jerking away from the door as though it'd turned into a hot stove.

"Hello, Duchess." The face that smirked back at me through the bars was one I'd hoped never to see again. Not that Loki was a bad puss, as things went, except where he wasn't much of a cat at all, for all that he had four legs, a tail, and a proper spine. He never smelled quite right, too much Human on his fur, too much dog on his breath, and his sense of humor was too rough for a self-respecting Tuxedo.

Plus, there was the unavoidable fact that where Loki went, chaos followed. Which was fun to read about in the papers, but not so much when it was your own life.

"You working for Dumpster now?"

He gave that the scorn it deserved. Loki worked for no-one save himself, and I wasn't even sure about that. Work wasn't Loki's thing, not unless it made trouble for someone else.

"I can just turn around and leave you here, if you'd like?"

"Loki?" Sammy squeaked again.

"Hush, kitten," I said, leaning one shoulder against Sammy's. He let me. When you go whisker to whisker with an actual Mistoffelees, even an alley cat could understandably get spooked.

I stared into Loki's pale blue eyes. "What's the catch?"

"If I said there wasn't one, you wouldn't believe me."

True enough. "So, just out of the blackness of your soul?"

A twitch of the whiskers, there. "And because it will annoy Peaches, of course."

There was a rumor that they were litter-mates, Loki and Dumpster. If so, their mother's womb should be scoured with fire. Loki smirked at me like he knew what I was thinking, his patchy white markings making it look like someone had spat a mouthful of milk in his face.

If they had, nobody would blame them. Or have heard from them again.

"I think I hear the clitter-clack of little thug claws heading our way," he said, those pale blue eyes holding mine. "You want to be here when they crawl in, or do you want to be gone?"

Sammy might have been able to slip the lock. But we'd still have to get past Dumpster and his guards. If Loki was offering us an out, he meant all the way out. "Gone. Please."

If he caught my hesitation between the two words, it didn't bother him. There was a slick noise, too wet to be a lock pick, and the kennel door swung open, Loki taking a step back before it caught him.

Sammy bounded past me, through the door, and then did a

perfect hindquarters turn and dashed back past me, into the kennel.

"Loki."

Unlike Sammy's earlier squeak, Dumpster growled the name, an underlying hiss making my skin twitch, the fur on the back of my neck ruffling in reaction. I felt the urge to follow the tiger back into the kennel, but forced myself to stand my ground, trying to keep both males in my line of sight.

Dumpster had turned to face Loki, the flex of muscles under that orange and cream fur seemingly overmatching Loki's smaller form. Loki seemed to think so too, backing up until his forepaws touched his hind. But the low warning rumble that came from his throat was anything but cowed.

Dumpster took the challenge, a matching rumble and flattened ears trying to show Loki who was boss here.

"Boys." I packed everything I had into that one word, all my annoyance and irritation, and wrapped it up in a bow of exasperation with posturing children.

They kept their gaze locked on each other, nose to nose, but the growling faded a little, and their years twitched, proof that they were listening to me. Then Dumpster eased back, and Loki spent half a minute carefully washing his ear, nonchalant as though the other tom hadn't just threatened to kill him.

No fight, then. Not yet, anyway.

Dumpster rolled his eyes when Loki switched his attention to a paw, carefully cleaning between sharp white claws. "Why are you poking whiskers into my business?"

"Because your business intrigued me. You've hired more brutes and paid them enough to keep 'em quiet. Tsk." Loki looked up then, practically waving a reproving paw in Dumpster's face. "And then these two sneaky pusses go in... and they don't go out. It was almost as though you were hanging a sign — 'come Loki, come take a look!'"

Dumpster's tail swished once, barely-controlled irritation. "Someday you'll run out of your last life, and you won't be able to borrow another."

Loki looked past him, at me. "The thing about curiosity and cats? People only remember the first half of it. The second half is what's important. 'Curiosity killed the cat... and satisfaction brought her back.'" He tilted his head, and spoke directly to Dumpster, then. "But you wouldn't know about satisfying a queen, would you?"

There wasn't any warning, no fluffed tails or arched backs or the high-pitched growls young toms think make them sound tough. Just a burst of muscled fur and a cream-colored paw knocking Loki on his ass, blood welling up through his fur.

Even as I was telling myself that Loki could handle himself just fine in a dirty fight, that I should be grabbing Sammy and beating claws out of there, I'd leaped, aiming for what I thought was Dumpster's rump.

They'd squirmed to the right before I landed, though, and I ended up catching a paw in the face. No idea whose, and at that point I didn't much care. I wrapped my paws around the thick cream-colored neck and latched down with my teeth on the nearest ear, yanking hard.

That worked better on kittens Sammy's size. Dumpster shook me off, and turned, ears flat, mouth open, his tail a straight line behind his back. He didn't see a source of information or amusement, now. He saw an interloper he wanted to kill.

"Shit."

I wasn't going to back down, though. Not with Sammy still in the kennel behind me, and Loki down for the count.

"Come and get it," I growled, my own ears tucked out of claw-reach, muscles tensing and ready to leap or turn, as needed. My tail lashed once, then stilled. "Or can you only perform when your audience is locked up?"

Someday, my mouth was going to get me killed. Might be today.

------

Maybe there are some kits who don't learn how to fight past the usual rough-and-tumble from your littermate, but if so, I've never met one, and I'm pretty sure they've never made it Alleyside. My claws might be filed short but that didn't mean I couldn't use 'em, and I'd yet to meet a tom who could pin me unless I wanted him to.

That didn't say it was going to be easy. Dumpster outweighed me by a considerable amount, and was meaner, and smart didn't stand a chance against that. But I had a kit to defend, never mind he wasn't mine. I let him think he was going to get my throat, and closed my jaw on the soft flesh of his hind leg. A clench and a pull, and there was a sweet, sweet howl of anguish in my ears, before he twisted hard enough to knock my head against the floor. Concrete hurts. But I didn't let go. I'm not sure I could have at that point.

Anyone who says "cat fight" in dismissive terms has never seen one. We posture a lot, but once we have teeth in, we don't intend to let go until someone is bloody and defeated.

Unless, of course, someone turns the hose on.

"Whadda ya know, 'madder'n a wet cat is an actual thing," a voice said, the mockery tapping like claws on cold tile, dry and precise.

I spat tufts of fur from my teeth, shook water out of my eyes and glared in the direction of the speaker, but had enough smarts left not to attack. Dumpster wasn't so lucky, and by the time I could see again, two barkers had him down on the ground, and were reading him the Act about assaulting a police officer.

Meanwhile, a lean, bright-eyed Kuvasz named Wolfgang was grinning sardonically at me, the butt of a stogie hanging from his jaw. He knew better than to light up, but the stink of it made his soft white fur a disgrace. "Wet pussy, my favorite."

I shook myself, quietly pleased when the drops reached him, and he flinched. "You done yet?"

Wolfgang pretended to consider that for a minute. "Nope. But the boss wants to see you. Upstairs."

His boys were already rousting Dumpster out the door, so I whistled for Sammy and followed Wulfie's fluffy white ass up a flight of concrete stairs.

Neither Sammy nor I mentioned the fact that in the chaos, Loki had disappeared. If Dumpster said anything, the cops weren't listening.


I'D BEEN RIGHT; we'd been in a sub-basement of the house. The cement stairs led to the side alley, which consisted of a surprisingly nice patch of catnip running alongside a low stone wall that might have been pleasant in less unpleasant surroundings. I could hear noise coming from the front: at least two squad cars, and a shelter wagon, possibly hauling away Dumpster's goons even as I breathed fresh air again.

A striped shadow slipped past us on the stairs, and I held my breath, but nobody hauled him back by his scruff, or called a warning to anyone at the door. If Sammy'd learned anything, he'd push paws the hell out of here, and not look back until he reported in to Momma.


SPARKS WAS WAITING in the alley. He nodded once at Wolfgang, who nodded back, and followed the other barkers around the corner of the house, giving me a hard clip on the top of my head as he went. I hissed, and his chuckle drifted back to me.

I kinda liked Wulfie, most days. Except for the stogie.

"You okay, Duchess?" Sparks' concern sounded real, but there was a glint in his dark eyes and a smirk on his muzzle that suggested he maybe was enjoying my waterlogged state too much.

"I've had better afternoons." I sat down and tried to lick my shoulder dry, then gave it up as a bad job. Sometimes, the only way to maintain your dignity was to ignore anything was wrong.

"I've had worse. You're to thank for that, so consider this my thank you."

The voices out front kicked up a notch. Someone with a good set of lungs was annoyed at "neutered bullies going where they had no right on private property." I got up and padded over to take a sneak around the corner, and saw a couple of patrol hauling unmarked file boxes out down to the street, along with the goons. Three squads, and two wagons from the shelter. They'd come loaded for bear, like the Human said.

I ducked back before anyone, pro or con, could catch my whiskers. "You got a warrant?" I was pretty sure they'd gotten no such thing.

Sparks raised one eyebrow like he'd invented it. "Patrol was keeping an eye on this place, heard what they considered to be calls of distress from within, and called for backup."

I'm not a big fan of supporting cops in their lies, but on the other paw, we *had* been yelling for help, so maybe one of those flop-eared woofers *had* heard us. Less plausible things have been possible.

But my life, I've noted that possible and plausible pretty much always give way before premeditation. My tail twitched, and my ears lowered.

"You were following me. You saw me go into the house —"

both of us carefully ignoring the fact that we'd obviously been doing some B&E of our own — "and decided to use me as a claw to pry open the door." I wasn't sure if I was offended they'd assumed we'd need rescue, or annoyed he hadn't just *asked*.

Sparks let out a bark of laughter. "Don't flatter yourself, kitten, you're not that special. But I'd hate to see you get chased up a tree before you could help me."

Right. I'd promised that, hadn't I? Or heavily implied it, anyway, which to Sparks would be the same thing. And now he was going to try and collect.

"This," and my ear flicked to indicate the house behind us, and the circus out front — "isn't enough help? You forget how to catch your own prey, desk-boy?"

I could tell him I didn't have anything, that the entire case had been a bust-up. If his boys had gotten through fast enough, they might even have gotten hold of the files I'd seen, gotten him enough to hold Dumpster on suspicion, long enough to build a case to hold him for a nice long haul in a kennel all his own, not quite so nice as the one he'd locked us in.

But what I'd said before about plausible and probable didn't hold for toms like Dumpster. He was too slick, too sleek; he hadn't built up this much of a power base without the claws to protect it. Claws that weren't his, that couldn't maybe be traced back to him.

Sparks still needed me. And he might give me some rope to run on, but he wasn't going to let go of his end, not until I gave him something he could use. Not once I'd told him I planned to *get* something he could use.

Sometimes I wanted to go back and slap past-me soundly across the ears.

"You really wanna make me chase you, Duchess? Because we both know how that ends."

I looked over his shoulder to where Sammy was perched on

the wall, trying to look like he'd just wandered by on accident, just a random kit on his first life, checking out the commotion. His eyes were wide, his tail low and curled around his backside, the tip twitching in fascination. He'd managed to avoid the water, managed to avoid the barkers, but Sparks knew he'd been in there with me, if he'd gotten reports of us going in. Did Sparks know Momma's eyes were still on us?

Didn't matter: I knew. And the second law of the Alley was, you don't tell the dogs anything, and you never gave up one of your own, no matter what.

"Come on, Duchess," Sparks said, his eyes dark and sorrowful the way only dogs can do, damn their domesticated genes. "Right now I can toehold Peaches on unlawful kenneling. But you know as well as I do that there's not a judge around that'll be able to make that stick. Not with you being you."

"Excuse me?" But he was right. A puss off the street, even the Alley, might have a case. A puss who made it her business to poke whiskers into other folks' secrets? They'd assume I'd done something to deserve it, say he was only protecting himself, and it wasn't as though I'd gotten hurt, so lick it off and move on.

Way of the world: Dumpster slept in better laps than I did, and everyone in this alley knew it.

***

It was full dark by the time I made it back to my office, pushing the door open just wide enough to slip through, rather than letting it swing wide enough to bloody the nose of anyone standing behind it. I didn't bother turning on the lights: there was enough moonlight coming through the windows for me to make my way to my desk, one nail unlatching the bottom drawer where the day-cleanser was hidden.

Although 'hidden' was a nice way of saying it was tucked

between the bills due and the bills paid folders, in plain sight of anyone in need.

It burned nicely going down, and I wiped the mustache off my whiskers with a tired sigh, letting the bottle clink down on the surface of my desk as I crawled into my cushion, and only then spoke to the other presence in the room.

"It's done." I reached down and threw the files on the desk next to the day-cleanser. "But you knew that already, didn't you?"

"I heard a rumor." Boomerang Took padded forward, still as sleek and sweet as the first day I'd seen him, whiskers quivering with uncertainty. But his eyes were fastened on the file on my desk.

"Yeah. You have friends who like to listen to rumors, don't you? Did they tell you I talked to the dogs?"

All it took was a few words, and Sparks had enough to yank a few prominent tails, get one of them to yowl a name. He'd get his promotion, and me? I'd get known as the puss who rolled over to get her belly scratched.

Or the one who'd gotten played by feathers on a string.

"You were in it from the start, weren't you." It wasn't a question. "The only thing I don't know is, if you were a pawn Sparks decided to use, or you like being a woofer's chew toy."

"I didn't lie to you." He glanced up at me, then away, and if I'd been a softer puss I might have bought the hint of desperate shame in his eyes. "But one of his dogs caught me outside the club, said they'd seen it go down, they knew a way out of it, but I had to do exactly what they said. I couldn't let the cops get involved!"

Took was a fool of a puss, but that didn't make him a bad puss. Just ripe to be used by a dog looking to make his mark, and a beat-up PI needing to make her rent for another month or three.

"They have enough to make a case without you," I told him, shoving the folder across the desk, and watched as his entire body eased, whiskers drooping in relief. "Go home, puss. Stay home. They Alley's no place for you."

They Alley was no place for any of us. But that's where the work was.

And Sparks *owed* me, now.

## SPARK TO TINDER

It was my first month on patrol. I was the tenderfoot, meaning
I got the shit calls and the bad shifts. Still, it wasn't all bad. Met
interesting people, ate in a lot of...interesting diners, and the
brass mostly didn't pay attention to what we were doing, so long
as we kept our noses clean and our receipts in line. And you met
some interesting people, three am in a shitty neighborhood.

It was a Tuesday, my partner and I had just finished booking
a john who'd decided to beatdown a deadbeat client. Normally,
my take is let the scum take each other out to the curb, but in
this case the femme had gotten caught between the two of them,
and they'd sent her straight to the morgue, do not pass go and
absolutely do not collect your two hundred dollars, or whatever
her going rate had been. She'd been called Jenny-dots, and she'd
been a good-looking bitch, bright-eyed and curl-tailed, and she'd
always had a soft spot for the woofers who worked her block.

So taking down the dogs who'd done her in was the sole
bright spot in that night's shift.

My partner Dickie was greying around the muzzle, but still
stocky and strong, pure bulldog down to his claws. "Pup," he
started in on me, and never mind I was full-grown; to him I was

forever going to be working on my milk-teeth. "Pup, ya gotta learn how to leave the job on the job."

"Yeah Dickie, I know." I'd been getting that speech for a month straight now, ever since he decided I wasn't going to wash out and might some day make a decent cop.

"You don't, some night you're gonna put the muzzle in your muzzle and blow your damn fool ears off," he went on like I hadn't said anything, also as usual. "So don't."

"Okay, Dickie."

If Dickie'd been able to leave it on the job, he wouldn't be stuck shepherding a noob on the shittiest shift in the shittiest beat. But I didn't say that. I just pushed my coffee back and forth between my paws and waited for him to finish.

The waitress behind the counter was giving us a once-over; she didn't mind us being here, particularly this time of night — the uniforms warned off the rats and junkies — but she also wanted to close up and go home, and she couldn't do that while we were still sitting here, nursing discounted-but-not-freebie coffee.

"Come on, boss," I said finally as Dickie started to wind down, his jowls flapping with unselfconscious earnestness. "One more pass round the block, see if we can find someone thinking impure thoughts, so you can yell at 'em."

It was midwinter, and anyone with a smudge of sense between their whiskers were either home, or taking shelter. I could feel my claws trying to retreat into my paws despite uniform-issue wools, and for the first time I envied Sergeant Cal. Yeah, his fur was a pain in the ass during the summer, but the Malamute didn't even feel the cold.

But as bad as it was for me, Dickie had to feel it worse. You'd never know, though, to watch him. He moved slow and steady down the street, jowls swinging as he checked out everything without being obvious about looking at anyone too long. I hadn't perfected that yet, and there were days I didn't think I ever would.

But I was still the one who saw it.

"Hey." I didn't approach too close: the first thing you learn when you put on the uniform is that seventy pounds of muscle and muzzle is going to look intimidating no matter how soft you pitch your bark or how low you tuck your body, and you can't tuck it too low or some alley stray is going to think you're going submissive and get stupid. But I did settle on my haunches, ignoring the ice-fucking-cold cement of the sidewalk, and brought my head down, neck tucked and ears forward, just like they taught us in academy. "Hey, little guy. You okay?"

Sometimes, they scurry back and run. Sometimes, they creep forward. And sometimes, they launch themselves claws-first at your nose.

Thankfully, the ball of fluff wasn't strong enough to do real damage, and I managed to extract it from my face without too much damage to anything other than my dignity. Dickie, busy laughing his balls off, was no help whatsoever.

On closer inspection, my assailant was a half-grown tabby, sleek but too skinny, with fur puffed up to twice its size, and a tail that could do damage as a lash, if I let it get close again.

"Lemma go! Lemma go! Police brutality! Help!"

"Sweetheart, you attacked us," Dickie said, getting his giggles under control. "I don't think that's gonna fly." But he glanced around anyway: some alley rats don't need truth to make trouble if they think they've got a shot at us. The cold worked in our favor: the one poodle down the street was more interested in getting into a car that glided up to the sidewalk, and had no interest whatsoever in okaying attention to us.

My momentary distraction got me a hiss right in the whiskers, and the sweet-sour breath made my nose wrinkle. "Kid, relax," I said, putting them on the ground and keeping them in place with one paw on the back of their neck. The puss didn't want to tay put, but instinct made their body flatten in response, and an unhappy little whine came out of his — no, her, I decided — throat.

"You got a name, kid?" And son of a bitch, Dickie had me doing it now, too. "You alone? Your momma around? Sibs?

I got another hiss in response. From the look of her, grey fur matted and thin, her tail longer than her body, she was still a kit. The Alley wasn't kind to kits who didn't have littermate. It wasn't kind to those who did, either, but at least then I'd have someone to hand her back over to.

"We can't leave her here," Dickie said. "And I'm not taking a wee puss like this down to the station."

We'd had a terrier lose his shit in the holding cell last week. Even with juvie cells, it wasn't safe for kittens, and keeping her in the squad room wasn't much better; they weren't bad dogs, as a rule, but some of them had never gotten house trained, not to put too fine a point on it.

"Shelter's not much of an answer, either," I shot over my shoulder, keeping a careful eye on the tabby. She'd subsided for now, but I didn't trust the meek surface for an instant. "KWS?"

"Fuck. I hate dumping 'em into the system, but yeah. At least they'll make sure she's fed up and gets all her shots."

"No!" For a little thing, the puss had muscles under the scrawn, and a jolt of adrenaline to drive 'em. She had gotten out from under my paw and was halfway gone when Dickie caught her by the scruff with his jaws, like she was one of his own pups. Her legs flailed, but she couldn't do any damage. From her language, I revised my estimate: she'd been in the Alley for more than a few months.

"Careful, she probably has fleas."

"I do not!"

"So she does speak. Put her down, Dickie, she's not going to bolt again, are you, sweetheart? There's a bowl of chowder in it for you, if you behave."

Her tail twitched once, hard enough to break a bone, then she sighed. "Yeah, okay."

---

I'D GIVE this much to the puss, she had dignity, even with bulldog droll on her fur. Put some food in her, she'd maybe grow up to be a sleek little looker. If she didn't end up scarred or maimed, like most of the Alley.

She could also put away salmon chowder like she a tiger. Although food in her mouth may have been her excuse not to answer any of the questions Dickie was trying to ask her. No name, no family, no life story such as it was.

"What does any of it matter?" she asked finally, regal in her disdain. "It's not like you'll remember past this table, and nobody else cares, either."

"Because..." Dickie floundered. He was used to street-toughs and professional criminals, not wayward kits, and I could see him realizing that his bark-and-cuff method of raising bulldog pups wasn't going to go over well, here.

"Look, little duchess," I said finally. "You're right, we aren't gonna remember, probably. But being in the system, however shitty, is better than being alone."

"No it's not." She half-lidded her green eyes at me. "What did you call me?"

"What?" It had slipped out, I hadn't even been thinking about it. "Oh, Duchess? You've got that 'tude, that sniff down your nose arrogance, I guess."

Dickie snorted, like he'd never watched a single episode of Downton Abbey — he totally had, I knew that from his missus — but the tabby turned the word around in her head before finally nodding. "Okay." She put down the spoon, and licked her whiskers clean, then took couple of laps of her water. "Thanks, boys," she said, and then the little minx was off the vinyl seats and out the diner's door between the legs of a pair of startled humans.

"Son of a...." Dickie started to swear, then sighed. "You think we're gonna end up picking her up for vagrancy, or worse?" he asked, staring out the window like she might come back to give us the finger.

"Probably," I said, reaching for my wallet to pay for the three bowls of chowder, and two coffees, then stopped.

My wallet was gone.

"Check your badge," I said.

"What?" He did so, and the expression on his face probably matched mine when his hand came up empty.

"On the other hand," he said, "she may end up doing just fine."

---

THE PUSS HAD BEEN RIGHT, mostly. Not that I forgot about her, but mostly I didn't think about her, washed over by all the other hopeless cases and lost souls who fell into the Alley and became my job, one way or the other.

Two years later, Dickie'd finally gone stomping off into retirement, and I was breaking in a noob of my own. I tried not to call him kid, but it was hard. Beagle was still wet behind the earflap, and I was pretty sure he'd end up shooting himself before he ever nailed a perp. But I was doing the best I could.

We were filling out paperwork at the end of the shift when

the night sergeant waved me over. I tossed the last of the papers to the kid, and ambled over to see what was what.

"You sponsoring a hawkshaw now, Sparks?"

"What?" It had been a long week, and I was tired, but I was pretty sure Willoughby had just asked me — "No." I didn't have any use for private cops, and I sure as hell wouldn't have vouched for one.

"Yeah well, some puss just put in paperwork and named you as a character witness. You want I should kick it back and tell them to take a long walk off a short pier?"

"Gimme that." I took the application from him, and scanned the filled-in lines. My eye scanned the name, dropped down to the employment history and bill of clean legal and moral health, then dragged back up to look at the name again.

"Clear it."

"You sure?"

"No. But do it anyway."

I handed him the papers back, and went back to my desk.

"You good, Gord-o?"

"Don't call me that" the beagle muttered, his ears flopping sadly as he tried to make heads or tails out of the arrest report I'd tossed him. "Was this mook trying to hire the hooker, or beat on them?"

"Sometimes even they don't know," I said. "We go with whatever costs 'em more. Look, Gord-o, I gotta book early. You got this?"

He waved a paw absently at me, not looking up from the form. "Yeah, whatever, go see your girlfriend or boyfriend or bookie, whatever. I'll be here, slaving away, busting my ass to make your ass look good."

"You're going to make a fine cop some day, Gord-o."

"Yeah fuck you, just go already."

THE ADDRESS on the application was deep in the Alley. Not surprising, really; cheap real estate, and if you're in bad enough shape to need a PI, you probably don't have money to hire someone on the Street. But every jack I passed could tag me for a cop, and there wasn't anything I could do about that: too many years on the force changes how you walk and stand and, fuck it, probably how I breathed, too. But for all the sideways stares I got, nobody was interested in making trouble for themselves, either. They sidled away when I passed, and I did them the favor of not looking at them when they did.

I wasn't here officially, anyway.

The building wasn't bad, as Alley hole-ups went. Brickwork was solid, windows were intact, lights were working, and the front door had an actual lock as well as a row of seven placards next to each ringer. Seven names, seven offices — I looked up and double-checked — three floors. Two offices to a floor, and one in the basement, maybe? Or someone was pulling down serious greenbacks and took the entire top suite.

Then again, this was the Alley. The first floor could be more expensive — easier to slip out the back door than to drop out the top window.

I squinted at the placards, aware I was dithering and irritated at myself for it. Third down from the top, there it was.

I rang the buzzer for the fourth one down.

"Yeah?" Male voice, raspy, accent of someone who didn't grow up speaking English, maybe-probably eastern European.

"Lemma in, wilya?"

There was a pause, then a buzzer sounded. I have no idea why nearly everyone does that despite knowing it's stupid, except maybe down here most don't have shit to lose. Or they just don't care any more.

I didn't wait for whoever it was to come down and check on who they'd just let in: I slipped inside the building, and let the door close completely behind me with a reassuring snick.

The lobby was large, maybe half the length and all the width of the building, with a row of brass mailboxes on one side and a beat-to-hell staircase on the other side, and a door at the back with a sign on it that read "private." If I'd been here on official business, I'd be opening that door first, without bothering to knock.

I took the stairs, alert to every sound and smell. The steps were covered in cheap carpeting the color of bad puke, but that didn't do anything to muffle the clang of the metal underneath. My ears were pointed forward in a way that my ex said made me look, and I quote, 'ridiculously adorable,' the better to catch the echoes ahead of me, but other than a muffled argument as I passed the second floor, the building was silent. Either nobody was home, or they were all dealing in whispers.

Fourth floor. Gentlemen's collars and ladies' perfumes. I pushed open the door, and took a whiff.

Maybe not perfumes, but not bad. Someone had left a window open, or used air freshener in here: it smelled like ozone and clean fur rather than the half-expected dust and mildew. I'd been right: there were three doors along the hallway, solid wooden things that looked newer than the walls and floors. Each one had a placard next to it.

I walked down, keeping my steps as light as possible on the grey-tiled floor. First placard: Bennefeld and Astro, Bail Bonds. Second placard: Malloy, psychic advisor. I snorted.

Third placard was cleaner than the first two, the paper stock still white rather than finger-grimed grey, and the edges were still square in the holder, not crumpled or bent.

Duchess, Private Investigations.

I sniffed once, quietly. Cat dander and wood polish, stale coffee and...

My whiskers twitched, and I felt my muzzle curl back a little. Reheated salmon chowder.


I LIFTED MY PAW, and knocked once.

# THE CASE OF THE FECKLESS FERRETS

It had been a quiet day going over the books, until Sammy burst into my office without so much as a knock, tossing a folded newspaper on my desk. It landed heavy, like fish a half a day from going bad.

I eyed the folded print with disfavor.

The half-grown puss managed to check himself before he followed the newspaper onto my desk, sitting down on the guest cushion with a thump.

"Didja see?"

I assumed he meant the newspaper, not his less-than-graceful entrance.

"This isn't your den," I said calmly. "You should knock and wait for permission to enter, unless something is at your tail. Is something at your tail?"

It was entirely possible. Sammy was one of Momma's wayward kits, which meant trouble stuck to them like cream to whiskers. And since I'd made the mistake of using him on a case a few months back, Sammy seemed to think any trouble he got into was something I should get into, too. I'd yet to make him understand that I only deal with trouble that pays.

Sammy was a smart kit, at least where his own fur was concerned. "Sorry Duchess, wasn't thinking, won't happen again."

I believed that as much as I believed it would rain sardines on Sunday. Common sense and experience got together and told me to tell him to take his newspaper and his excitement and march it back out again.

But he was still staring at me with those damned round kitten eyes, his ears tipped forward and the tip of his tail quivering, and there was a very real chance that if I ignored him, he might explode. I'd be willing to take the risk, except I'd never get my deposit back on the office if it was splattered with catgut.

I reached out to flick open the newsprint. The full headline, revealed, wasn't any better than I'd expected.

FECKLESS FERRETS FOIL THE COPS!

My whiskers pulled back slightly in amusement. "It must have pained them horribly that the Feds didn't come down to poke around, to give them alliteration." I looked back up at Sammy, who didn't seem to share my amusement. "And you brought this to my attention, why?"

"You're not even curious?" Sammy sounded as affronted as his half-grown body could hold. "C'mon, Duchess, this is the most excitement we've seen in weeks!"

My whiskers pulled back, and an ear flicked. "We're not the ones seeing the excitement."

He kept staring at me.

The facts were all over the Alley by now, but I skimmed the article anyway, in case the reporter had accidentally stumbled onto something new. A big-money house party two nights ago: all the creme de la creme of society attending, four-footed and two — and a few without any feet at all — gathered to celebrate someone's something or other with all the glitter and glam the Street could muster, which I'd been informed was considerable.

And at some point, during the evening, everything worth pawning had been placed and picked off the wearers without their noticing, from watch fobs to wallets.

But only the males.

"Feckless, but not rude," I noted, tapping a claw on that paragraph before moving on. And not stupid — males were far less likely to notice — or admit — that they'd been pickpocketed.

As expected, the reporter didn't know anything more than anyone else did, they'd just printed it up prettier.

Nobody had seen the thieves, of course. But the paw prints left behind in the flowerbeds outside the estate were a calculated — and familiar — taunt. Ferret paw prints, clear and unmistakable.

Sammy was practically quivering from tip to tip while I made a show of considering the evidence.

Or that lack thereof, really.

Home invasion, robbery, females untouched, males skimmed for all they were worth. It didn't take Woodward or Bernstein to figure out whodunit. The gang the news had quickly dubbed the Feckless Ferrets, for both their arrogance and their (assumed) species, had struck before. Seven big ticket thefts in the past three years, each with the same MO, and each time the cops had been left with nothing in their paws except embarrassment. And a lot of insurance companies had to pay out considerable kibble.

There were the usual conspiracy theories that the paw prints were a facade to throw the cops off, that it was actually a gang of squirrels, or magpies, or some other known thieves, that it was actually a gang of humans, even that the heists were planned by the victims themselves to rip off the insurance companies, but most folk with common sense ignored those. General wisdom was that ferrets were the only ones with the stones and brains to pull this off, *and* the ability to mingle without being noticed. Squirrels couldn't help but be rude, and magpies were born to attract attention.

"Nice haul, they got," I said, finally. "Not that anyone up there is crying over their lost pretties. I'll lay odds every Street puss in the room is dining out this week on the story of how they were brushed up against by a notorious criminal." And eating up the jealous sympathy they got from their peers. Call me cynical, you wouldn't be wrong. "The loss of a few shiny toys is nothing, compared to that."

"Who cares about them, Duchess," Sammy said, finally losing patience. "They're offering a reward!"

"They've been offering a reward for two years," I said, abandoning the newspaper and curling back on my cushion. "You know why nobody's collected on it yet?"

"Because nobody wants to be a rat," he said, with the prompt cynicism of Alley born and bred.

"We'd rat our mothers for half of what they're offering," I said. "But nobody knows anything worth the reward. Because whoever they are, they're smart. Very smart."

"But you're smart," Sammy said, and then his tail stilled, like he hadn't intended to be that obvious.

"Smart enough to stay out of it," I agreed.

"But — " Sammy practically bit his tail before anything more escaped. Tigers tended to be impulsive, but he'd been in Momma's care since he'd been weaned, more or less, and while she might be mostly interested in their less than licit skills, she hammered in survival tactics, too. And right up there in the top three had to be "don't backtalk your elders if you don't have an escape route already planned."

"Did you expect me to dive in whiskers last, or were you hoping I'd agree to help you?" It could be either: Sammy had picked up an unfortunate case of hero worship after that blackmail case, once he'd gotten over getting side-eyed at close range by both sides of the law, but he was also a puss with an eye for his own self-interest, and the reward for information leading to the capture of the Ferrets would set him up on the Alley for at least three of his lives.

Sammy shrugged, reaching out to snatch the paper back with one claw, folding it and tucking it under one leg. "Both? Either? Whatever worked."

I liked him better when he wasn't trying to golly-whiz me. The wary, ambitious kit with a skill for B&E I'd first met was one I could work with.

Not that I was going to, in this particular instance. This was a matter for cops and payback companies, not a singleton PI who worked for a retainer up front, thank you very much.

"Scat, cat," I told him.

I listened to the office door close, Sammy's tail whisking through just a second before, erect in the air, with only the faintest quiver at the tip letting me know he wasn't as offended as he was playing.

I shook my head, and groomed my whiskers, thinking about the article. Truthfully, the case had piqued my interest. But not enough to chase after an invisible string in the hopes that there'd be a mouse at the end of it.

That wasn't my gig.

The problem was, there wasn't much else happening just then that was my gig. Sure, I'd gotten some work in the aftermath of the blackmail case; some folk must have suspected me of selling out to the woofers when Dumpster went down, but there were enough who either trusted me, or were desperate enough not to care. There always were, that's the one certainty of a PI's life. But the other certainty is that no job lasts forever, and there will always be downtime, when the bills still gotta get paid.

I had two messages on my desk, both of them hunt-and-peck

jobs. Follow the cheater, catch the cheater. Then hope that your client didn't take their fury out on you and refuse to pay once you showed them the evidence.

I hated hunt-and-pecks. But the retainer from either one of them would cover me for the rest of the month, and maybe a little longer, if I ate flounder rather than filet.

Someone came up to my door and stopped outside. My ears flicked forward, but I waited. Might be someone pausing to read the sign by the door, looking for someone else. There was a CPA down the hall who got a we-don't-talk-about-it amount of foot traffic.

But they didn't move on. I head feet shifting, claws clicking against the tile flooring.

"If you had a warrant you'd already have come in," I said, raising my voice just enough to be heard through the door. "But never let it be said that I wasn't a hospitable host."

A bark of low laughter, the door swung open again, and two woofers came in. The first was a heavy-set Labrador who'd seen the hard end of a few sidewalks, followed hard on his haunches by a younger, slightly less bulky Shepherd.

"To what do I owe the owner of a visit, Captain?" We had a history of under-the-mat favors being exchanged, but normally when Sparks wanted something from me — which, admittedly, wasn't often — he had one of his woofers play fetch. The Lab with him today had done the job a time or two, actually, and had never been happy about it. For Sparks to come down here...

I leaned forward, flexing my claws once, then sheathing them before anyone noticed. "What do you need that they can't know about down at the station?"

"Now, Duchess..." Sparks took the cushion opposite my desk, settling himself with dignity. The Lab stood against the wall, his butt parked in parade rest. Ex-Coastie, I'd bet. You can always tell the guard dogs.

"I'm sure you have a reasonable and non-condescending end to that sentence," I shot back, and had the pleasure of hearing his long jaw click shut. One of these days he'd bite his tongue when he did that. I didn't even feel the need to be there to witness it; it would be enough to know that it happened.

"How about we start again from the top?"

Now I knew he wanted something from me. Sparks wasn't bad, as woofers went, but he still wore the uniform, and being polite was something they saved for the Street citizens, not us down here in the Alley.

"Be my guest," I said, and took up my hearing-the-client-out position; ears forward, tail curled and still, whiskers forward, eyes wide. It was a facade and Sparks, unlike most of the idiots who pad through my door, knew it.

He declined to take the bait, which told me whatever brought him down here, it was serious.

"I'm assuming you've heard about the recent dance up on the Street this week."

"Mole rats in Sing-Sing have heard about the dance," I retorted. "Must be embarrassing, getting slicked again by those boys."

The Lab growled, low in his throat, but Sparks didn't take that bait either; he really wasn't any fun to play with.

"I want to hire you."

Well. That was not what I'd been expecting to hear.

---

If possible, the Lab looked even more unhappy once Sparks dropped that bombshell. Clearly, he didn't think this was a good idea, but woofers had pack mentality down, and where Sparks led, the Lab was going to follow. At least until he caught enough rank to fight him about it. But for now, he settled for crossing his pawns across his chest, and glaring at me.

I've been glared at by better.

Sparks didn't look much happier, if I were being blunt. He wasn't what anyone would call a mellow dog on the best of days — someone'd strapped his harness too tight when he was a pup, and he'd never quite gotten used to it — but every line of his body said, "I don't wanna talk about it."

But he was the one who'd come down here, so he could either say it, or just sit there like a log.

I waited, then made a show of reaching for the paperwork on my desk, shuffling them into a more-important looking pile. "Gentlemen, I realize you're on the taxpayer dollar, but the rest of us have to work for a living. So, if you'll excuse me..."

"I said, I want to hire you."

"I heard you. But lots of people want to hire me, and very few actually do so. Hire me to do *what*, is the question you need to answer next. Because I'm reasonably certain you've got a whole station full of patrol ready to jump when you bark, right?" I narrowed my eyes at him. "Or is this something you can't let your boys in blue know about? Oh, Sparks, I'd be so proud of you if you're finally getting your paws muddy..."

"Bite me," he growled, but there was a resigned smirk to the curl of his lip, and I relaxed a little. Despite what I'd said, I didn't want to see Sparks go dirty. It would be like finding out Santa did side work as a stripper: nothing to be ashamed of, but slightly depressing to watch.

"But you got that much right. This isn't something I want barked around the water cooler. You're more useful to me in the shadows. But this is a legit deal." His left ear twitched, something I'd learned over the years meant he was amused about something. "Cash, no trail, nothing to tie you to us."

"Or you to me," I said, intrigued despite myself. "So, you're bypassing the usual suspects" — a well-placed detective agency the local woofers usually palled with, when they needed stuff outside their yard — "to work with little old me. Because I've already proven I'll hand over all the details without haggling?"

"Because you won't hold back anything that might actually be relevant for later bargaining," he corrected, and all right, that was a fair catch. I hadn't told him everything with the last deal, but to be fair, he hadn't been paying me for that either.

Money changed things.

"Something you want kept quiet, something that you think I can help with more than your Street sniffers..." I narrowed my eyes at him again, my whiskers pulling back as my thoughts were derailed by something unpleasant. "This had better not be about the Casifer incident."

The Lab growled again, and even Sparks had an involuntary twitch in his muzzle. None of the woofers liked talking about that, or even having it talked about. Can't say as I'd blame them; if that was what Sparks was here about, I'd do it, but it would cost him. A lot.

"No. I want — we want," he corrected himself, "you to put your very specific skill set to use in regard to the recent incident we discussed earlier." He made a face as the words came out, like they left a bad taste in his mouth. Someone else had put them there; that kind of political ooze wasn't a Sparks thing, not even when he was bucking for promotion. So, I decided to help him out, 'cause I'm a hell of a puss that way.

"You want to pay me to go poking in the muck you boys can't get traction in," I said. "Find out the chatter in the darkest shadows of the Alley, and trot back to deposit it like a mouse on your mat."

"Yes."

No. Oh, seven hells, no. "You think I'm not already in deep enough for being a stooge, after our last go-round? When you made a point of using me to do your dirty work, and then leaving me to hang?"

"It took you all of a week to talk your way out of that." Sparks had perfected the art of being deeply unimpressed, at least when it came to back-Alley PIs. "This is on the clock and under the table, Duchess. Don't play too hard to get, or you won't get got."

Like he had anyone else to go to, down here. But I took the warning.

WE SET it up the way these things generally worked: once Sparks left my office looking pissed and muttering to himself, I was officially on my own. If anyone asked, I'd told them to take a long leap off a short pier.

Unofficially, I was now a sub-contractor to the local woofers.

It had been a hell of a Monday.

THE FIRST MISTAKE new meat makes, in the Alley, is thinking that they should play it cool. There's this idea out there that not wanting anything means you'll get what you really want.

Everyone wants something. Looking like you don't is just asking people to dig, to find out what it is. No, the trick is, go in with an agenda. Tell them up front what you want. Tell them what you're willing to pay for it.

And then, when they're trying to break you down in price, you look for what it is you *really* want.

I slept on the new gig, hoping that something brilliant would come to me overnight. Nothing did.

I made breakfast, then cleaned up after myself, did a quick

grooming, and found myself contemplating my nails, wondering if it was time to get them trimmed again.

Procrastination. It's not a good look on any cat, least of all one with a paycheck to earn. I'd made it clear to Sparks that I was being paid on effort, not results, but I had to show I'd made an effort.

---

"WELL, well, well. Look what the cat herself dragged in"

"Yeah, you're a laugh riot, General." I slapped a paw down on the counter, just for the joy of seeing the old tom flinch. It might not be nice, but General brought that out in me. He was ancient. Alley gossip guessed him to be at least nineteen, maybe older, and he'd been in a fair number of brawls, not all of which he'd won. All that had just made him nasty rather than wise. But he still ran the best damn bodega in the Alley, and always had the freshest catmint. I wasn't dumb enough to get hooked on the 'nip, but catmint took just enough of an edge off that I could focus.

"More than you usually take," he noted. "Something's got your tail kinked. Tell grandpa about it," and he leered at me, like I'd be willing to go belly-down for him.

"In your pitiful dreams," I shot back, sliding coin across the counter, and taking my packet. "The only thing that's got my tail kinked today is that I have to work for a living. I made bad choices somewhere along the way."

"So say we all," General groused. He scratched at one mangy grey shoulder, then shook his head roughly, ears flattening. "All I'd need is one lucky ticket..."

"Or a nice heist," I agreed. "What do you think a share of this weekend's Street heist would bring an honest puss like ourselves?"

"Nothing," he said grimly. "Honest pusses don't get shares of anything like that. It all goes to the smarter ones."

"Smart enough not to get caught, anyway. Not that the woofers have a clue."

"Don't you get caught up in that," General warned. "Not that I care what you do," he added. "But you're a steady customer, and you're no worth to me dead."

"Every one of my lives is precious to me," I assured him, and left the shop with a little more than I'd come in with, including my catmint. Whoever was behind this, the General thought they were more than just clever thieves. He thought they were dangerous.

---

I took my 'mint and went down to the Library. I'm not much for book-reading, but there was a park out back with benches that caught the afternoon sun. It was a good place to knead and think. Most of the benches and cushions had already been taken by the time I got there, but a steady stare at some of the younger ones, and a prime spot opened up. I made a show of brushing their fur off the sun-warmed plastic, then settled myself, tail curled over my rump, chin resting on the lip of the seat and the 'mint under one paw. It was better once the sun'd warmed it a bit, anyway.

It took about four minutes before my lure caught its first squeaker.

"You sharing?"

"Depends." I opened one eye lazily, taking in the scrawny puss in front of me. "Are you?"

"Depends. Whatcha needing?"

"Whatever's hot." Even if the squeak didn't know anything about the heist, no bit of gossip was ever wasted.

"Council's gonna vote on the crows tomorrow, word has it they've been paid off to ignore the whole roost."

"Interesting, but not unexpected. Gonna have to work harder."

"Doxy just got scooped up by a Streeter."

That got my second eye open. Doxy had sworn she'd never leave the Alley. Still, she was getting older. A soft cushion and two steadies a day sounded good, after a couple-three lives pounding pavement. I might go that route myself, some day. Maybe.

"More interesting, and unexpected." I cut a pinch of the 'mint off and offered it. The squeak took it with a surprisingly gentle paw, like he hadn't expected I'd actually give him anything.

"That was a pity pinch. Gonna have to impress me, for more."

He wanted to give me more, I could tell the way his paw trembled, and he couldn't quite pull his claws in all the way. But he didn't have anything.

I almost gave him another pinch to go. But that wasn't the way this went.

---

THE REST of the afternoon was more of the same: I picked up some dirt that I could certainly put to good use, if I were of that bend, but nothing and I meant nothing that even whispered about the heist. And it wasn't the 'I'm not breathing a word, or I'll end up whiskers-deep in cement' kind of silent, either. Nobody knew nothing.

I closed the bag of 'mint and tucked it away, drawing myself up into a comfortable thinking-perch. It was more common for everyone know a bit of something, even if they were wrong, than it was for nothing to be known. That told me two things. One: these ferrets were pros, which we'd already been assuming, and two: General was probably right about them being dangerous. Because the only way you kept this kind of silence was if you killed off anyone who knew.

Well, anyone who knew, who you couldn't keep a leash on, anyway. And that made me wonder about General some more. How much did he know, and could I convince him to tell me any of it?

Probably not. But I'd keep him tucked into my back pocket, if things changed.

Half of the PI job was sheer, you should pardon the expression, doggedness. But some of it was a purely feline ability to sit quietly and think. I spread my left paw and groomed between my pads, letting the familiar, soothing motions free my brain to work.

Competent, quiet, and dangerous. The second mistake new meat makes is thinking that dangerous means making a lot of noise, of making sure everyone's got your name between their jaws, fear of you masking their claws. They forget that the most effective hunters are the ones who don't make noise until *after* they catch their prey, and the deadliest don't make any noise at all.

There was a thump on the seat next to me, and I tilted my head to look at the newcomer.

"Whatever you're selling, no."

"Why you think I'm selling?"

"Because that's all your kind do."

"That's slander! Or racist. Probably both."

"And horrendously stereotypical, but tell me I'm wrong."

The badger showed its teeth — all there, all sharp, yep — but didn't tell me I was wrong.

"Tell me something, Tugger. If you wanted to pull a job and

didn't want anyone to know anything about it, either before or after, how would you do it?"

"Hypothetically?"

"Hyp — yes. Just between us mammals."

I got a snorted opinion of that. "I'd tell them they don't get paid until we were done, and then I'd kill them."

"Yeah. That's what I was thinking, too."

"You got something planned?" Its ears perked. "Wanna let a pal in on it?"

"Just hypothetical."

"Whatever." The badger patted a pocket invitingly. "Sure you don't wanna — "

"No."

I didn't know something without shoulders could shrug that eloquently. "Your loss, sister."

FERRETS HAD a reputation for being fast and sneaky. But they were also smart. And they gossiped like bees on a honey bender. If one of their own was killing off helpers, that would get out no matter how fast the dead were offed, and our masterminds would lose future helpers quicker'n a cabbie can run your charge.

So, what was the smarter alternative?

I had no idea. But I thought I knew someone who might. If she'd talk to me.

"RITA."

My winning charm and sweet smile didn't win the puss over. She stared at me from around the edge of the door, one paw curled into the frame hard enough her claws were leaving dents, the other out of sight. From the tendrils of smoke rising from near her hip, I was guessing she was holding a cigarette, not a gun.

"You know those things'll kill ya," I said.

"It'll have to take a number and get in line. Duchess. Been a while."

"You told me to get out."

"First time you ever listened to me."

"You were holding a butcher's knife."

She'd turned away by then, so I couldn't tell if she was rolling her eyes. She probably was. I followed her inside, closing the door behind me.

Her place hadn't changed; a surprisingly comfortable remix of trashy glam with an emphasis on glossy pink. It was already giving me a headache.

"You still palling around with the Human?"

"Occasionally."

That had been one of our major disagreements. Rita didn't hold with mingling with Humans, and I didn't buy any of her arguments against it. I wasn't about to take a collar, that wasn't my scene, but I wasn't going to diss anyone who did, either. Life's hard. If you decide a warm lap's better than cold brick, more power to ya, and the Human had never tried to scritch my ears without an invite, which put them a couple up on most of the Alley already.

The thought occurred that I could have asked the Human about this case. They'd given a push here and there, before. But that had always been at their instigation, meaning I owed them nothing for it. Best leave it be.

She settled herself on one of the pillows, not pink, but a dark rose that set off her black and fawn fur perfectly, lean limbs arranged like she was about to be immortalized as an Egyptian statue.

"So why are you darkening my doorstep, Duchess? Not to reminisce about the bad old days, I suspect."

"If I were, would you be interested?"

She took a long, studiedly obnoxious drag from the cigarette, plumes of pale grey smoke escaping from between her slightly-exposed fangs. "No."

The difference between a wise puss and a dead puss is knowing what rats not to chase. I ignored the stink of her cigarette trying to climb down my throat, and groomed my tail, waiting.

"You want something I know." Rita laughed. "All right, ask. Worst I can do is not tell you."

"The gang that's been shaking down Street parties. They local, or out of town?"

It'd been a shot in the dark, more hope than proof, but the way Rita's eyes narrowed, my pulse jumped.

"Or maybe the worst thing is, I do tell you," she said. "Duchess, you sure you want to poke around in this? More important, why you wanting to poke around in this? Curiosity kills smart pusses like you."

"And satisfaction brings me back. People always forget that part. My own wondering, Rita. It's a slick job, no mistake, and I'm wondering who has the whiskers to pull it off."

"No other reason? You not looking to chase down that reward?"

I turned my tail twitch into a scornful swoop. "I could think of better things to do with the information than go to the woofers."

"Yeah? Like what? Cut a piece of their action?"

If it was anyone else, I'd have maybe gone in with that move. Wouldn't be the first honest PI lured in by the sticky-salt smell of easy lucre. But Rita knew me too well; she'd smell shit before I'd even laid it down.

"To my everlasting regret, I'm too honest a puss to scratch at that. My life would be easier if I weren't. But I also admire artistry, and everything I've seen of these heists tells me they're artists. And, to be honest, I hadn't thought ferrets had it in 'em."

"Guess they do."

Rita knew me a long time, but I'd known her just as long. My ears twitched at the same moment my whiskers trembled: it wasn't what she'd said so much as how she'd said it. Layers and shadows and implication heavy as cream.

"Doll, what's going on."

The moment I asked, I knew I'd made a mistake. Rita was a dame down to the bone, and like any dame she was bad news. So far, I'd been able to play her good side to my advantage, but as the cold muzzle of a gun slid against my spine, I was pretty sure I was going down for the count.

"Sorry, doll," she said, and there may have been regret in her voice. "But a puss has to take care of herself, right?"

And then the lights went out.

---

I WAS DREAMING of rooting in the back alley behind a decent Indian restaurant, hoping to find some of the Masala I could smell before something bigger and meaner came along. As dreams go, it wasn't all that bad, even if I'd sworn years ago never to dumpster dive ever again, so I was slightly irritated when the sound of click-tic-click-tic dragged me out of the dream, slowly emerging into awareness.

"She's pretty," a voice said, tight and high.

"She smells." A different voice.

"They all smell," the first voice said. "She's still pretty."

I was awake enough to hear voices that weren't dreams. And awake enough to realize that the sensation of a small hand petting me wasn't a hallucination at all. More: there was the weight of a collar around my neck. I managed to keep my instinctive hiss clamped between my teeth. Generally, if someone's petting you, they're not about to hurt you. Generally, not always.

I live in an enteral haze of hope.

In addition to the collar, I was also blindfolded, I determined, feeling the press of cloth against my eyes and whiskers, the weight of a knot under my chin where I couldn't shake it off. Rita. Or someone else who knew how easy it was for us to slip out of most anything. I flicked my ears, an involuntary expression of disgust, and the paw that had been stroking me fell away.

"She's awake." I'd been right, that was pro-pretty.

"So, guys, I'm gonna — " Rita. My ears went forward, and my tail lashed once, before I got control back. The hiss I'd held back before escaped, though.

"Doesn't sound like she's too happy with you, cat." A third voice, but all of them had the same high-pitched squeak to them, like they'd been partying with balloons most of their lives.

"Yeah well, she'll get over it. We're good now, right?" I couldn't sense anything, but my ears were working fine: Rita was unhappy, not about flipping the dime on me, but about being where she was, wherever we were. Nervous, and not sure she was getting out of here. Not reassuring, Rita. Who'd you hand me over to?

"Yeah, we're good." A fourth voice, okay. Four around me, plus Rita. More? I couldn't tell but I thought so. Something about the voices...

There was the click-tic of claws on flooring — hardwood, or tile, I thought — and the sound of a door opening and shutting.

Suddenly the smells and sounds of my dream made sense. Rita'd dumped me in the middle of what I'd been looking for.

Ferrets.

A fifth voice — softer, lighter, chirped in: "What do we do with it?"

"Excuse me. Not an it." It might not have been the smartest thing, sassing people who had me collared and blinded, but there were certain indignities I wasn't putting up with. "Name's Duchess."

"Pleasure to meetcha, Duchess." That was Stinker, showing he could put up manners as good as mine. Not that that was saying much, but hey, it was the effort that counted, right? Three speakers, but I was reasonably certain there were at least five in the room, from the scraping and shifting I could hear. If my whiskers were free, I could have located them all, individually, but they'd known that. Or Rita had told them. What was Rita doing with a gang of ferrets, anyway, and why had she flipped me to them?

"I'd say the pleasure's all mine but really, it isn't. Mind undoing the bondage gear, at least enough for a girl to breathe?"

"Don't" a voice called out, while another, bitingly, told the other to chill his panties. That set the lot of them off, and I upped my estimate to maybe seven or eight in the room, or at least with opinions about what should be done with me.

"Kill it," a voice said, overriding all the others. "Rita should have done it for us, if the puss was that close, but what she can't do, I can, even if the rest of you are chickenshit."

That set off another round, this time arguing over who exactly was chickenshit, with a sideline into what made people think chickens were so timid, had they ever actually *tried* to take down a rooster?

If I wasn't certain the last voice had been deadly serious — me being what would end up dead — I'd have been amused, and more than a little bemused. This was the gang that pulled off such sophisticated, slick heists? Really?

"Killing's messy." That was... Stinker, I decided, and also decided that he was if not the leader, than at least a lieutenant, because they all settled down after that. I decided I'd forgive him the smell comment. "We can't afford mess, not right now."

"We can't let her go, either. Not now." That was Not-Chickenshit, and if it hadn't been me he was talking about, I'd have been agreeing with him. I had enough of their voices to recognize them in a dark alley now — well, assuming they said anything. That made me a liability. But between killing and letting me go...

Uh-oh.

"So, what, we stash her in the back room with the Dixie cups and plastic forks?"

"We make her useful, like cups and forks."

Yeah, that had been what I was afraid of. When the blindfold came off, I was tempted to keep my eyes shut, like if I didn't look at them, they'd have no choice but to drop me on a street corner somewhere, alive and limbs mostly intact.

I'd never been that lucky in my life.

When the blindfold finally came off, and my eyes adjusted, I was alone in the room with a single ferret. He was leaning on the back of a chair, paws crossed under his chin, studying me. I got the feeling those beady black eyes didn't miss much, if by 'much' I meant 'nothing.'

"Name's Rascal."

Rascal was... well, he looked like every other ferret I'd ever seen, not that I'd seen many. White chest, black mask over his eyes, blackish brown fur down his back and on his paws, long nose and an impressive set of whiskers that right now were twitching in my direction.

"Where'd your friends go, Rascal?"

"Things to do, events to arrange. I thought we could have a nice private chat."

"Lucky me. What're we chatting about?"

"About how you get home in one piece, all your body fluids still contained in that pretty little shape of yours."

Ferrets might have a better rep than most, but they're still weasels.

"You want me tied up in whatever you're planning, so if I squeak on you, I'm cutting my own whiskers off, too."

"Pretty *and* smart. I almost want to keep you past your expiration date. You've got two choices, long-tail. One, you play nice with us, and everyone goes home clean. Two, you get a tied-up sack and a lesson in how to swim in it. What's it going to be?"

A better puss would have spat in his face and told him to do his worst. A smarter puss would have played for time, figuring they'd find a way out of the mess. Me, I'm a practical puss. Sparks would disavow and deny any knowledge of what I was doing and any connection to his beloved department, but he also wouldn't let me take a complete fall, if I gave him the ferrets, too.

I just had to stay alive long enough to get the goods.

"What's the game plan, boss?"

RASCAL MIGHT HAVE ACCEPTED my word, but he wasn't taking it for granted. I had a companion assigned to me — "your training buddy," he said with a grin. Koko wasn't thrilled to be paired with me, either, but the grey-muzzled ferret took his orders with glum resignation. At least he hadn't been the one who wanted to dump me in the river. I'd take what I could get.

I looked around the room I'd been brought to, without actually taking my attention off Koko. A kitchenette against one wall, and a long table at the other end with eight chairs pulled under it. Assuming they used this as their dining room, which seemed reasonably logical, there were at most six others. Or way more than that, and they ate in shifts. Everything in the kitchenette had been put away, which surprised me: I'd never thought of ferrets as being particularly orderly. Pretty much the opposite, in fact. Then again, I suppose the ability to pull off large-scale heists on a continued basis said *someone* was thinking logically.

Koko reached out and poked me in the chest with one claw. "So, you good for anything, long-tail?"

"My skills are varied and at a higher pay rate than yours," I shot back, and Koko cackled into his whiskers. "I doubt that," the ferret said. "But hey, show me what you got, hotshot." He pointed me at a pile of locks, and ostentatiously pulled out a stopwatch.

I was no Sammy, but my claws hadn't lost their touch. By the time I had the last lock open and placed neatly on the table, Koko was looking, if not impressed, then at least no longer resigned.

"Nice touch," he said. "I may be able to do something with you after all."

It wasn't that easy, of course. Locks were just the start: then it got physical, often with Koko snapping commands in a soft voice I had to strain to hear, and not listening wasn't an option when at any given moment those commands might be all that kept me from a nasty shock — literally, since some of the tests were wired — or getting my flank whacked with a narrow but nasty lead pipe that appeared in Koko's paws when I didn't move fast enough.

By the time Koko finished with me, my fur was matted with sweat where I couldn't reach to groom, and even my whiskers were sore. My sole consolation was that I'd nailed every test, including the high-window shimmy I was pretty sure he thought would stop me. Ferrets think they're the only ones with a wiggle in their tailbone. If I'd been a Rottie, maybe... but a Rottie would never have gotten herself in this mess, and if she had, they wouldn't have offered her a way out.

Flexibility isn't just in your spine, and a cat worth even one of her lives knows to a whisker what she can do.

"Congrats, pretty. You passed."

"Oh yay." I tucked my paws carefully and didn't give him the satisfaction of trying to groom the rough patches. "Now what?"

"Now you get introduced to the rest of the crew." He leaned forward to poke me in the shoulder, then danced out of reach when I took a swipe at him. "Come on, pretty, time's a wasting."

Be damned if I was going to be introduced to anyone, even a gang of miscreants — especially a gang of mistreats — looking like this. Playing on every stereotype of pusses ever, I sat my backside down and took a few good long moments to put my fur in order, best I could, and make sure everything was in order.

"Oh, for... come here."

I'd pegged him right. Koko took my head between his paws and made sure the fur I couldn't reach was smoothed and slicked down properly. Up close, his scent was still aggressive, but less offensive. Or maybe I'd already gotten passing fond of him.

"Come on," he said, letting me go abruptly and stepping away as though to deny he'd ever been doing anything of the sort. I hid my grin and followed. Now, maybe, hopefully, I'd get some answers.

"Hey kids," he called out, as he ushered me through the

double doors that had previously been locked — I'd checked, when I thought he was distracted. They led into what looked like a classroom: a bunch of desks and chairs shoved to one side, clustered around a flip-board, the visible side covered in neat white chalk marks. I didn't have a chance to check what they said, though, because the bodies in the chairs caught — and held — my attention.

Three of the bodies were long, lean, and bandit-masked. No surprise.

The other three, though. Them, I didn't expect.

"Fleidermaus, Claude, and Clara. Minor, Tazar, Magellan." He clocked through them all, every one of them straightening when he said their name. It was like watching military roll call, if the military took ferrets. Or Poodles.

Nearly half the visible, introduced Feckless Ferret gang were dogs.

And one catnapped puss.

RASCAL'S BRIEFING WAS, well, brief. I wasn't given the chance to ask questions, and I was reasonably certain they wouldn't have gotten answered, anyway.

"You'll work this one in pairs, same as before. Claude, you're taking our newest member. Teach her the ropes."

Claude, the apricot Poodle, eyed me with distaste, but didn't protest. A small, reddish-coated ferret, did, with an indignant "Hey!"

"You're sitting this one out, Minor," Koko said. "Don't give me gruff; your leg's still not a hundred percent."

And there was my answer to how they were getting past security guards and bouncers. The places they were hitting, ferrets wouldn't even get in as hired help, but nobody in the flash neighborhoods looked twice at a well-groomed Poodle, even if their invite wasn't a hundred percent.

I'm not proud of how it is, but that's how it is.

I hung back when the others filed out at the jerk of Rascal's paw, looking at Koko. "You aren't coming with?"

Koko snorted, pushing me out the door where the others were already loading into a white-paneled van that had pulled up just outside. "Old men get to mind the fort." He didn't sound too depressed about that.

Minor — a reddish-brown ferret with startling blue eyes — sulked off to the side, arms crossed over her chest. "She better not get my share, too."

I was about to offer to stay behind, just to make her happy, when:

"Everyone gets paid," Rascal snapped, backhanding the smaller ferret none-too-gently as he walked past her. "So long as they don't question my decisions."

Minor glared at me, and I glared back, until Koko put a paw between us, and nodded at the van. "Get going, puss. Try to have fun. I'll see you when you get back."

Koko reminded me of Momma, the puss who took in most of the strays in the Alley, taught 'em mostly-legal skills, kept 'em out of jail or gangs. They weren't good, by any stretch of the word, but I wasn't comfortable calling 'em bad, either. Very little was that black or white, when it came to what you did to survive.

I knew that, firsthand.

The inside of the van was surprisingly comfortable, with low, padded benches and straps placed for standard Poodle-sized comfort. I eyed the space, then slid onto one of the benches before the black Poodle, Fleidermaus could claim it, curling onto the seat with a glare when the bitch tried to nose me off.

"Gotta be faster than that, stiff-nose," a ruddy-coated ferret — Magellan, I thought — cackled at her, and reached up to high-paw me.

I slapped back, watching as the ferret scurried off to claim a space for himself. Shades of shadows, I reminded myself. Yeah, they were thieves, and yeah, they'd talked about killing me, but I knew plenty worse.

Claude was the last to get in the van, before the doors banged shut, and the engine started up. "Hey, partner," I said, trying to make the best of the situation.

He stepped carefully over to me, looking me up and down like he was trying to decide if I was worth the effort of sneering at. So much for that, then.

"Hey, it's not like I asked to be here," I said. "Can't we at least try to get along?"

That got me narrowed eyes and a deliberate rump-turn, spoiled by the van taking a sharp right turn that slid Claude sideways and into Clara, a little brown ferret, who snapped at him before climbing up onto the seat next to me, curling herself into tight ball, and going to sleep.

I envied her that ability: every muscle I had was quivering with tension, and maybe yeah, a little fear. I wasn't going to kid myself: I was in well over my whiskers right now, and no idea how to get out.

The van was paneled, which meant there were no windows for me to grab some landmark or sign that would tell me where the hell we were, and since I had no idea where we'd been, it's not like counting turns or even time of travel was going to help me any. No idea where we'd been, no idea where we were going, no real idea what I was supposed to be doing once we got there, except trust a dog who clearly hated my guts to 'teach me the ropes.'

Maybe Clara had the right idea after all. I settled myself

more firmly on my square of cushioning, tucked my tail over my nose, and concentrating on getting my nerves to settle and my muscles to relax, starting with my tail and working all the way up to my ears.

If you can't make a plan, go with the flow, and maybe something will turn up.

There wasn't much chatter; I studied the others in the van through half-slitted eyes, trying to see if there was anything there I could use. I didn't think they'd been working together all that long, or maybe Poodles just naturally fussed more than ferrets. Claude and Tazar, a slightly smaller black Poodle, were deep in conversation, looking over at me every now and again, while both ferrets occasionally woke up long enough to yawn and look around, then go back to sleep. Rascal had disappeared through the sliding door between the back of the van and what I supposed was the cab, while Fleidermaus was off in a corner by herself, glaring at the ceiling of the van like it had mortally offended her.

It wasn't just me then: she hated everything.

About ten minutes in to the ride, the door slid open again and Rascal slid through. That was a signal, I guess, because Tazar grabbed a kit from under the bench and the Poodles started loading up on the accessories: expensive-looking collars and nail-gems, plus a dousing of fur-sparkle that left the rest of us coughing. Pale pink powder settled on my fur, and I gave everyone a dirty look on principle before grooming it off.

Sparkle-powder tastes like crap. For the record.

Since nobody offered me pretties, I went the groom-and-prep route, smoothing down my fur and making sure my claws were in good shape. My manicure was a disaster, but you didn't want to leave polish behind if you had to scratch in deep, anyway. Next to me, Clara stretched and yawned, this time staying awake, looking like she'd never done anything more criminal than steal a q-tip.

"All right, children, listen up. Kitten, you too." Rascal leaned against the divider, beady eyes glaring at all of us in turn. "Two-hour window, full room. Target's ground floor, so if something goes wrong, we do a fast flow and meet up as usual. Duchess, don't even think about doing a runner in that case; we will find you and we won't be happy."

His voice was calm, almost cheerful, but I didn't doubt the violence in that promise for a second. As cute as Clara was, ferrets were stone-cold killers. Ask any rabbit.

"Nothing stupid, boss, got it. Do I get to know where the usual meet-up is?"

"Follow one of us."

Great. The onus was on me to stick with them, and I had my doubts Claude would stop long enough to make sure I was on track. Whatever. The day a Poodle could out-sneak me, I'd turn in my whiskers.

"Here." Speak of the devil: Claude shoved a square cream-colored card at me. I took it carefully, between two claws. "You're going in on your own four. Try not to open your mouth too much; this is a high-class scene."

The "bite me" that came up my throat stayed locked behind my teeth.

The ink on the card was a deep blue, minimal flourish, requesting my attendance at the exclusive opening night preview for Rusty G's first exhibit in eleven years.

My whiskers lifted in surprise. Even I'd heard about Rusty Guy; he'd made a splash on the scene when he was barely weaned, critics raving about his ability to weave art deco delicacy with brutal neo-modernism, and that was a direct quote. I'd never been able to figure out what the hell that meant, but the few pieces I'd seen had suggested that Guy's head was an unpleasant place to be. The fact that he'd put so few originals up for sale, and then disappeared for a decade had made the pieces highly sought-after, though, which meant that the gawpers at a preview would be high-end merchandise themselves.

Appropriately decked out with shiny, valuable trinkets, no doubt.

"Stick with me, don't do anything obviously stupid, and follow what I say. Koke says your slight of hand's decent."

"Decent enough." I'd swiped what he set out before his ruler could come down on my paw, anyway.

"Great. You're acting as bag." In case I'd thought that was some kind of slang, he handed me an actual bag, a pretty little blue cloth thing with brass studs and snaps that felt heavier than it should have: without checking I guessed there was a false bottom, probably false sides, too.

"I give you something, you stash it without anyone seeing. You manage that?" The look on his face suggested he doubted my competence and resented the lack thereof.

"I have no desire to be caught with stolen goods on my person," I said, and took the bag, sliding the strap over my shoulder and chest like a messenger bag.

And then the van stopped, the doors opened, and the first pair slipped out, ferrets curled around their Poodle's neck like the tackiest of high-priced status symbols.

"Thank you for not making me do that," I said to Claude, who let out an actual bark of laughter, and gestured for me to precede him through the door.

Maybe this wouldn't be so bad after all.

---

IN ANOTHER PLACE AND SITUATION, I might have enjoyed the

shindig. Not the art — Rusty Guy was clearly going through some kind of angsty period nobody needed to see detailed in paint — but for someone in my line of work, people-watching is both a professional skill and a hobby, and this crowd was a masterclass in expensive boredom mixed with a smear of middle-class pretension.

I leaned closer to my unwilling companion, lowering my voice not to be heard over the buzz of voices around us. "Please tell me we have no interest in any of the displays."

A snort of disgust was followed by, "Hell, no."

Claude and I were on the same page with our critical opinions. That was good to know. I scanned the gallery again. Maybe a hundred and fifty people, including the waitstaff, but it seemed to have an ebb and flow to it. Serious buyers came early, to look before the crowds got too thick, while the ones who wanted to make an entrance had to wait until there was enough crowd for an entrance. We'd slipped in during the downtime between. Made sense: the serious buyers weren't going to be as be-spangled as the later arrivals.

That didn't stop Claude from slipping me a wallet, oxblood leather and thick with cash and plastic. When I raised an eyebrow at him, the Poodle shrugged. "It was there, my paws were itchy."

"Do they have show ribbons for pickpocketing?"

That got me a glare in return. "Do I look like a show dog? We were hunters, originally. We need things to *do*."

Fair enough, I could respect that.

"So, am I leashed to your side for the evening, or can I wander?"

"If it was up to me, I'd have tied you in a sack and tossed you into the river. Keep an eye on me; if I look your way you have three seconds to take whatever I've lifted. Go too far and I'll assume you're trying to make a run for it."

I slid the wallet into my bag, and snicked the clasp shut. "Fine. Then I at least want something to drink." Turning a stiff tail on him, I flagged down one of the waiters bearing a silver-plate tray of something bubbly in flutes. I don't indulge in booze on the job, generally, but it would look odd if the two of us were wandering around the gallery glaring at each other, and neither one of us drinking.

The closest waiter bent low for me to snag a glass, and my gaze slid over the open top of his black vest to the glint of tech underneath. Wires, faint but visible if you knew what to look for. Huh. Either they were hot-miking their staff to pick up gossip, or this guy was security. Or, possibly, both. I'm paranoid that way; it's safer in the long run.

Could that help me? Maybe, if I could get Claude or one of the others to say something incriminating, without them incriminating me, as well. Fat chance. I smiled at the waiter and moved on.

The bright lights were making the tip of my tail twitch: I wasn't used to being anywhere so well-lit. The Poodles were circulating; I had no idea where the ferrets had gone to but suspected their bags of holding were larger than mine and getting heavier.

Rascal's plan was to lock me into their crimes, so I couldn't report on them without incriminating myself. It was a pretty good plan, and with anyone else it might have been enough to cow them into good (or bad) behavior. An officially undercover woofer could get away with pretty much anything, having the badge and paperwork to prove they were one of the good guys. My situation was... less clear-cut. The law was iffy on "under duress and working for the greater good" if you didn't have an official stay-out-of-jail card.

So I had to step careful: couldn't actively take anything, couldn't actively harm anyone... But mingling and occasionally accepting items from my "partner," that should be all right. I just had to make it through tonight, long enough to win a little room to breathe, and then slip out through... somewhere, with names and places and plans to hand over to Sparks, so he could do what he did.

That part was going to be trickier... For all that it had been fun and games once the blindfold came off, I wasn't underestimating this gang. They might be fluffy, but they weren't cute, and they weren't kidding. If I fucked this up, they would fuck me up

More likely, I'd end up in that sack in the river, sooner rather than later, no matter how well I behaved.

And even if I did make it out with names and descriptions... Sparks would still have to catch them. He couldn't put me on the stand. Or rather he could, but only as a hostile witness. Once I'd testified, my career would be over. I'd be reduced to marrying up-Street or leaving town entirely.

The thought sent a shudder running down my spine, all the way to the tip of my tail, which twitched once in reaction.

Damn it. I needed to stop taking these jobs.

I forced my tail still, ears forward, while I stared intently at one of the abominations on the wall as though considering how it would look in my powder room. I could pull a fire alarm and slip out in the confusion — that was a classic for a reason. But Rascal stayed with the van, so he could be anywhere now — and what about the driver? I had no idea who the driver had been. There was a player I didn't know, on the board. Odds of them being assigned to watch me: high.

When I got out of this, I was going to wring Rita's scrawny, self-serving neck. No, I was going to shave her scrawny self-serving fur and cover her with glitter, and drop her —

"Fern? Fern, is that you?"

The name sent my heart up into my throat before I throttled

it back down again. Breathe, Duchess. I wasn't Fern. Fern was long gone and — I'd thought — forgotten. Nobody should be using that name. Nobody should even *remember* that name.

I turned and stared up a long black muzzle into an oddly-familiar pair of wide-set brown eyes.

"You don't remember me, do you." The voice sounded less disappointed than worried. "It's Dominick."

No, it wasn't. It was Luc. Freelance muscle of the smarter type, good-looking enough to get hired to escort fragile but wealthy types when their regular bodyguards would be too obvious. Sweet, but with a left kick that could take down a solid wood door, and I knew that from observation.

"Dom. Right." I reached up to tap his nose gently, claws out just a hint. The fact that he'd used Fern's name meant he wasn't sure if I was on the job or not; the claws told him that yes, I was, and to be careful. "Long time no see. What're you up to now?"

He took a sip of the flute in his paw, his ear flicking backward to where a nervous-looking American bulldog was studying the canapé tray. I hadn't even known bulldogs could look nervous. Worried, yeah, they had that down to an art. But nervous?

So, he was here on a job. What was the bulldog up to — a meet? Or was Luc — sorry, *Dom* just hired muscle to protect the bulldog from the cohort I'd fallen in with? Or...

Didn't matter. Focus, puss, focus. I couldn't spend too much time talking, not unless I was also working, make it fast, puss, don't let any of the Poodles — or worse, one of the ferrets — see you talking to anyone.

Right now everyone is either an ally, or an obstacle. Use him or dump him.

"I wouldn't have thought this was your sort of thing." He indicated the art behind me with a twitch of his ear, and I took the excuse, turning so that anyone watching would assume we were actually discussing the... whatever it was.

"Oh, you know me; I go where the excitement is."

His pupils widened, and his nostrils flared, just a bit, exactly like I'd hoped. Dobermans were *so* predictable. "You're working," he said in relief. "Please god, give me something to do or I'm going to drown myself with this Bellini; my client hired me to protect his ego, not anything interesting."

"Not working so much as conscripted," I said, baiting the trap. "I was poking my nose into the recent thefts around town, which I'm guessing you know all about — "

He nodded his head, sipping his drink and scanning the painting over my shoulder, like he was already bored with what I was saying, good boy.

" — And they caught me."

Only excellent reflexes and good timing kept him from choking on his drink.

"You, they... they're here? I need to — "

"You need to stay put and stay calm, Dominic." I made his name into a whipcrack, low but sharp, and he settled back into his skin with a shudder.

"Right. Sorry. We'd split the reward anyway, of course. I would never cut you out. Um. They're watching you?"

"Us now, probably, yeah. Can you get a message to Sparks?"

Dom's ears drooped. "You mean, call him? Not even for my mother, sweetie. My client finds out I know the Cap, or worse yet he knows me, and I'm out on the curb, and he may be boring, but he pays well."

I couldn't exactly say anything about Dom's choice in clients, considering my own history — but just once, couldn't *someone* in this town be on the straight and narrow?

"Indirectly?" I gestured toward the painting, then shook my head in disgust. "If I twitch the wrong way, they'll be on me."

"Yeah. Yeah, maybe. There's a waiter I saw earlier, I know he's snitched before, mostly low-end stuff but they'll take him seriously. Maybe."

Maybe was better than I'd had before. I'd rather the message go from Dom to Sparks, less chance of something important getting dropped, but you worked with what you got.

"Right. Your attempts at conversation are starting to bore me, so I'm moving on now." I'd also taken his cufflinks as proof to Claude I'd been working; I figured Dom'd forgive me eventually. "High-sign when you manage to pass the message."

Dom rolled his eyes at me. "And what message am I passing along?"

I sat on the urge to be cute, or snarky. "That Sparks needs to get his rump here ASAP, before his wiggly little offenders slip back out into the night and take me with them."

Okay, I mostly sat on the urge.

As one of the waiters passed, I snagged a canapé with one claw, and turned away, my tail telling everyone how very done I was with that oaf of a Doberman.

And just in time, too, because Claude slipped through the crowd, draping an arm over my shoulder hard enough to leave bruises under the fur. "I thought I told you — "

"I got cornered," I said, opening my paw enough to show him the cufflinks, before I slipped them into the bag. That got a grunt of unimpressed approval, even as I felt something else small and heavy slip into the bag. I was well and truly carrying stolen goods, now. If the cops caught me, they might not stop to check with Sparks before tossing me in the slammer, and that was not a place I wanted to be, particularly. Especially not when, once they eventually got me out, the *why* of why I was getting out would spread, and same situation as testifying: Sparks is covered with glory, and I get the shaft. Possibly home-made one, sharpened to unpleasantness.

"You're thinking too much," Claude told me, making my ears twitch. "Go with the flow. This gig can be fun, if you let it."

Koko'd said the same thing. I was kind of afraid to find out if they were right. "You going to let me stick around long enough to find my groove?"

Claude was already scanning the room, nodding at people as though he knew them. "That's up to you, kitten."

"Don't call me that."

Ah, shit, we were falling into a buddy routine rap. Claude realized it in the same instant, and something in his spine stiffened. "Just look pretty and hold the bag, *kitten*."

Across the room, Dom was exchanging his glass for another with a waiter, whose ears were bent forward in an attentive pose: young dog to older of the pack issuing instructions. The snitch, I presumed. As though knowing they were being watched, they both looked up and — damn it, right at me. I looked away, deliberately, but out of the corner of my eye I saw Claude's expression change, and I cursed the fact that Rascal had picked Poodles, not Dalmatians, for his canine corps. They were too damn smart, the entire breed.

And nasty, as I learned, with seventy pounds of perfectly-groomed muscle showing me wet, black gums and very, very white teeth...

WHEN LAST WE left our heroine, she'd just had seventy pounds of pissed-off Standard Poodle getting in her face with his own. And while my jaw may be better suited for catching prey, his could do some significant damage to my neck, if he decided it was a thing he wanted to do.

I needed to convince him it wasn't. But that much hot breath on my nose was making it hard to think.

Black eyes rolled at me, the whites looking yellow up this close and Claude's growl sounded like the rumble of a freight train oncoming. "What did you do?"

"Careful, big guy." I kept my tail smooth, my ears forward, trying to be as low-threat as possible: I had no idea how much he'd figured out; he might have assumed a lot more than I'd actually been able to accomplish, or he might just be reacting on sheer gut suspicion and not actually knowing anything. "You know I'm not stupid, I'd be in the sack and breathing water already, if I were. So why don't you tell me what'd got your tail in a kink and we can get to the bottom of this."

It didn't matter what I said, just that the tone kept him from snapping his leash — metaphorical but possibly mental, too. Odds were decent Rascal had given all of them very clear instructions on what to do if I tried anything, but —

"Come on, think of the gig," I said, dropping my voice even lower, a co-conspirator's whisper. "Folk are watching." I was still keeping my ears and eyes focused on him, which wasn't hard when there were that many teeth gleaming in my direction. Poodles weren't scary on the surface, but when you strip away the curls and flounce, they had the same internals as a wolf.

And for all that I walked tall, I was about the size of Claude's head. He could snap my spine in two, if I gave him the chance.

Half a second ticked by while he confirmed that yeah, we were starting to gather a few eyeballs of attention. Timelines ran through my head, coldly brutal. Even if Dom had been able to pass the message, even if our snitch had a direct line to Sparks, or at least Spark's secretary, whose name I was blanking on, there's no way that they could get here in time. And unlike previous instances, even if he'd had someone tailing me to see what I turned up, we would have lost them at some point since Rita sandbagged me — and if not then we were going to have serious words about why they left me there. But no, can't count on the Alley's Finest, not in any time to be useful.

"So they're watching," Claud growled, and his muzzle dipped closer. "Give me one reason why I shouldn't slap a few lives out of you, anyway." His paw was large enough to do it, too.

"Right now, we look like we're having a spat. You make it violent, the gallery's security personnel will suddenly be paying attention, too."

I briefly considered letting him do it: if I timed my duck right, I'd still be conscious when they arrived, and could use them to make my escape. But no, he was here, and they were there and like the woofers, I couldn't trust them to be timely. Plus, if he did connect, a concussion would be the last of my worries. No, my best chance was to draw this out, and make him think there was no reason to get violent.

"You draw their attention, they might realize the invites we're holding are decent but not perfect fakes and start asking questions you don't want to have to answer."

The snarl eased back, teeth and gum-line no longer so disturbingly visible, but the look in his eyes hadn't changed. One claw-tip he didn't like, that look said, and he'd tear my throat open and leave the corpse behind as a warning.

Great. Rascal had teamed me with an apricot sociopath. Had anything gone right this week?

I wasn't dead. Yet. There was that. And he hadn't stopped to wonder why *I* didn't want security's attention, either. Again: either he had figured it out, or he was just acting on suspicion. I held my breath and hoped for the latter.

"Outside." The order was accompanied by a jerk of his head towards the side door, the one the staff had been using. Bad move on Claude's part; people would notice two guests using it. Proof that you could dress a dog up, but you couldn't take 'em anywhere nice.

But right now, being visible was a plus for me, within reason. Dom needed to be able to tell the woofers where I'd disappeared to. So I let him lead me out, for all the world looking like we're looking for a quiet place to have a knock-down claws-out fight.

Which we were, actually.

The side door took us through the space the caterers were using; I caught a glimpse of the snitch Dom had spoken to: he had his phone to his ear and his ears were pulled back against his head, making him look more like a rabbit than a pup. Not a good look on anyone, but fucking hooray he was making the call, assuming he wasn't calling his girlfriend or his bookie, first. And then we were outside, in the alley behind the gallery.

On second glance, it was decent for an alley, with cars parked along one side — staff, I was guessing, from the shitty makes and models. No sparkling bejeweled art patrons were driving a ten-year-old Honda — and actual working streetlights overhead, the dumpsters closed securely enough the smell was muted to a bearable ick. Yeah, as alleys go, this was pretty high-class. But the problem with nice alleys is, they've got fewer dark corners you can hide in. If I could get away —

I didn't get a chance to finish that thought, because Claude had me in a chokehold before the door swung closed, and he'd obviously been practicing on ferrets, because there was no way I was slipping free from that.

Muscle to muscle wasn't the only way to fight. I went limp, dragging on his arms, and protested, "I didn't do anything."

"Bullshit."

That wasn't Claude. Shit. I managed to open my eyes long enough to see Rascal in front of us, paws folded over his narrow chest, long face set in a disapproving scowl. When the hell had Claud called for backup?

My mouth hit autopilot, words tumbling out with enough

truth to — hopefully — be believable. "I swear. I ran into someone I knew, had to tell him something, get him off my tail. This is my town, I know half the fancy collars and all the alley-dwellers, odds of me running into one or the other was damn high and don't tell me you didn't think about that, you're smarter than that."

And I was an idiot not to have thought of that for real as Rascal's plan: someone would see me, someone would squeal, and the gang would disappear, leaving me to take the heat. And there was nothing Sparks could do to save me then, even if he was willing to risk his badge stepping forward. Because no matter how often we do good work, an alley-rat is always an alley-rat.

But I'd managed to put a claw in that, making a scene, maybe letting someone know I was here under duress.

"Job's blown. Finish her and get out of here."

Or, I'd just changed the story from fame-up of a pigeon, to frame-up of the dead pigeon. I let my muscles go limp, like I'd accepted my fate, flexing my claws in their sheaths as discretely as I could, when someone called, "Oi. What's going on here?"

The voice was raspy and belligerent and coming from over our heads. I knew better but looked up anyway.

"This is none of your business." Rascal glared at the shadow who'd spoken, and the shadow glared back.

"My alley, my business. Literally, my business." Three others appeared along the roofline, and there was enough light to see night-bright claws and gleaming golden eyes behind inky masks, long tails puffing up in a way that only a fool would think was anything other than a prelude to a fight.

"What do you have to say for yourself, puss? Should we come down and even the odds a little?"

I had no patience with gangs; no matter why they started out, they always went bad in the end, and left taxpayers to pick up the bill. But beggars and the badly outnumbered couldn't be choosers.

"If you would," I managed to choke out, before Claude yanked hard into my throat, and I could do no more than hack the rest of my words.

They'd only been waiting for an excuse, anyway.

Claude muttered something that would have gotten a mule's mouth washed out with soap, and dropped me, then dropped to all fours even as the door slammed open behind us. Three poodle-sized shadows rushed past me, taking up position shoulder to shoulder with Claude, even as smaller shadows flowed underfoot.

I dropped tighter to the ground, feeling the chill pass right through my fur and into my belly, the small blue bag an unwanted weight I didn't have time to get loose of, before I started to scrabble backward, wanting only to get out of the way of the inevitable fight.

That cliché about fighting like cats and dogs? The full saying is "fighting like cats and dogs until all that's left is fur and blood."

And raccoons fight like cats *and* dogs.

The thing about a fight — a real fight, not one where there's a lot of challenging and posturing but very little actual contact — is that they're *quiet*. You don't have energy to waste on hissing, and if you manage to blind your opponent with a well-placed claw or splatter of blood, you don't want to give away your position or intent with a yowl or growl.

So what you get is soft, heavy breathing, maybe a choked-off whine or rumble of anger, and the soft thuds of muscle against muscle and the narrow scrape of claws against pavement or bone. And if you're trying very hard to stay out of it, low to the ground and no making a sound at all, you can hear the faint rising howl of sirens, getting closer, before they were cut off suddenly, followed by the grind of tires on pavement and the soft slam of car doors.

Not in the alley, but close. It was too much to hope that the woofers had made it here that fast, but I hoped anyway.

Then headlights cut through the scene from the other end of the alley, and everything stopped for a split second, bloodied muzzles and flexed claws glinting, eyes dazedly blinking as they readjust to the sudden change in lighting. The shape behind the headlights was too big to be a squad car, unless they'd brought the paddy wagon.

Then a figure got out, too short and slender to be a woofer, and my heart sank. Not the cops. That was the van we'd used to get here. The gang was about to make a run for it.

Desperate, I rolled onto my side, risking exposing my belly to see if useful reinforcements had made it around the corner yet, gathering enough voice to warn them, ideally without getting a jaw full of teeth in my own neck or gut.

But the poodles seemed to have lost all interest in the fight, toenails clicking in a weirdly delicate sound as they stepped over — or kicked aside — the raccoon gang members, disappearing into the shadows behind the headlights and, I presumed, into the van itself.

Deciding they'd won, the gang declined to chase after them, instead letting out odd hoots that echoed against the walls, telling everyone within earshot that their territory had been defended. Great, goody for them. I tried to get to my feet, do something incredibly stupid like try and stop the van, or at least hold it until the woofers made it down the alley, and discovered one of my legs wasn't up to the task. Only then, when I realized there was something warm and sticky coating it, did it start to hurt.

A lot.

Damn. I flopped over onto my side, resigned and already

trying to figure out how to fast-talk myself out of trouble, assuming Sparks or one of his more trusted minions wasn't with the local cops, when I realized that not every fleeing shape was moving toward the van. A handful of shadows were flowing low to the ground in the direction of *away*, sliding right *past* the incoming woofers.

Little fuckers, I thought, half in admiration and half pissed-off. Team, allies, partners, my three black whiskers. They were leaving their slower, less sneaky canine cohort as a distraction, letting them be caught so the rest could get away.

I doubted that had been in the joint playbook. And that was why nobody trusted a ferret.

As predicted, the woofers raced straight for the van, and a volley of irritated barking ensued, the raccoons having already disappeared back up drainpipes and into the shadows of the roof like they'd never been there no sir not us. I thought about trying to tell someone that half their suspects had already escaped, then shrugged. They weren't going to catch them now; it could wait until I could talk to Sparks, make all this worth my while.

I hadn't counted on my tabby stripes being such a perfect blend: it took about half an hour and the chaos settling before someone noticed I was there.

"Hey, Duchess, 'zat you? Holy hoof, are you okay?" I paused in licking the blood off my leg to look up into the blood-shot eyes of a hound, his flashlight thoughtfully pointed down at the ground rather than in my face. One of the smarter woofers, then, or at least less of a tail-wipe. "Captain'll dock my ears if you're not okay."

"Nice to know Sparks cares. I could use some help, yeah." I might have a few more lives left, but I wasn't going to waste one being stupid, just to prove a point.

"How'd you get caught up in this — you know what, never

mind, I don't want to know." I still couldn't remember the woofer's name, but I recognized the face: I'd met him at the retirement party for Sparks' old partner, a couple years back. "Medic, we got a wounded warrior over here."

"Bite me," I muttered, but wasn't dumb enough to pretend I was going to walk out of there on my own four feet. The EMT, a burly, battle-marked Maine Coon, spent a few minutes checking me over before pronouncing a torn ligament and a bite mark that probably wasn't going to scar so long as I didn't do anything stupid, with the tone of someone presuming I was going to do something stupid. I would have argued with him except arguing with an EMT is pretty much the definition of stupid, thereby pretty much proving his point.

"Checked in with the station, Captain wants you to come downtown, give your statement." Smart woofer was back, and I could see the brass on his collar now, in the light from the bandage wagon, that said I wasn't the only one who'd noted competence. Poor bastard was probably going to make captain himself, before he was eleven.

"Statement, right." That was how we were going to play it, then: innocent bystander caught in the fracas when a heist went wrong. Nobody would believe it, but all that mattered was what went on the paperwork. So long as I still got my fee, Sparks could paper it however he wanted.

"Tonight," the woofer added, like there was any doubt about that. "You need them to give you a ride?"

The thought of being packed into the back of a squad car made my claws itch, for oh so many reasons. "I'm good, thanks."

"Suit yourself. You don't show up, that's between you and the Captain." He waddled away, shaking his head and muttering something about pusses it was probably good I couldn't hear.

I got to my feet, the bandaged leg holding me upright and

the shot of magic serum the EMT had given me doing the rest. I'd hurt like hell in the morning, but I'd worry about that in the morning. Reaching down I scooped up the small blue bag where it had been half-hidden under my body. It was tacky and sticky with blood — most of it mine — but everything inside was intact.

The temptation to keep what was inside flickered, a hot little flame of 'to hell with you, I *earned* this.' Nobody would know — they'd just assume it went off with the rest of the gang, never to be seen again until it showed up in some pawn shop three states away. But I had a code — not much of a code, but a code — and part of it was that I don't take things that haven't been offered to me, indirectly or otherwise.

Of course, walking back into the party — still going on, oblivious to the action outside, like good little rich folk — was out of the question, the way I looked. But this was the kind of Knight Errant and Gallant that Dom lived to play.

---

THE KITCHEN SPACE had calmed down, when I staggered back in through the door: they'd started to come to the end of their tray service, I was guessing, and now the bartenders were raking it in. The snitch pushed through the doors with two empty trays piled on one arm, saw me standing there, and I could see him trying to decide if he should drop the trays to help me, or drop the trays to run.

"Soften your tail, pal," I said. "Everything's been handled, everything's good." No need to mention any role he'd had in it: a snitch who's known is a snitch who's useless, and I wouldn't have put it past the ferrets to have someone on their payroll in the staff, too, just to cover their assets. "I need you to find my friend out front, let him know I may need some help getting home, though? I don't think I should go out there, looking the way I do..." I let my words trail off, until something spun and clicked in his brain and he handed the trays off to someone else, disappearing backwards through the door again.

"Oh, you poor thing." I wasn't expecting the hand that touched my shoulder, but the drugs in my system made me slow to react, when an older tom deftly turned me around and pushed me onto a low wooden bench, an icepack for my jaw and a stool for my leg appearing out of nowhere. "You knock heads with those bastard raccoons? I swear, they're a menace and we should just weed 'em out of the Alley. Here, have one of these," and he grabbed a canapé off a mostly-empty tray and shoved it into my paw. "Easy to chew but will warm your insides. Get me a cup of coffee!" he yelled over his shoulder, and I heard a muted "yes, chef!" before activity started up again around us.

By the time I'd eaten three of the salmon pate puffs and had a cup of seriously good coffee, Dom was standing in front of me, looking less worried about my injuries than he was put out he'd missed all the fun.

"Here." I handed him the bag, and he took it without question. "Some folk out there seem to have dropped a few things. Be a doll and return them for me, will ya?"

"And what do I tell the people who dropped things that aren't in here?"

"Check with the local lost and found. Maybe another noble soul turned 'em in." I doubted it, though. There was a reason the ferrets were the ones carrying the loot-bags, and it wasn't because they wouldn't match the Poodles' outfits. "And can someone call me a cab? I seem to have lost my phone." My wallet and keys, too, but there were ways around that.

Tonight: sleep in my own damn bed. Tomorrow, go down and spill my selected guts to Sparks. I doubted it would be enough to catch Rascal's crew, but knowing I talked might make them a little more cautious, send them to ground for a while. And without the mastermind in-hand, the Poodles would probably plead their way out, which meant I wouldn't have to testify which meant there was no reason to confirm to anyone ever that I'd been under contract, however unofficially.

But I'd still be able to collect my fee, for having tracked 'em down and successfully — mostly — spilled on their location.

It had been a decently good day, all things considered.

But next time Sparks called me down to the station, I swear, I was going to tell him I was in Tahiti.

# SCALES OF JUSTICE

*You want a story? One I haven't told before? Okay, so this is a story Duchess doesn't tell. It's not that she can't, you gotta understand. She was there for it, after all. It's her story, I just watched it all go down. And it's not that she'd be embarrassed to tell it, because if there's something that makes that puss blush, I ain't been blessed to see it.*

*But she doesn't tell the story, and that's a shame, 'cause, well, t's a good story . So I'm gonna tell it for her. And she doesn't like the way I do it, well, she can tell her her way, then.*

It was summer, the summer the bat house caught fire but somehow managed not to burn down, despite being fire-code-violating with the amount of guano they had settling in corners and places nobody should go. I'd been stuck in traffic on the corner of Seventh when I saw the flames go up, but it wasn't my job any more, so I let the younger bucks play hero. Saw the pictures on the news that night, though; a thousand bats squeaking and sweeping like they'd never been smoked out before. Pikers.

But anyway, it was that summer, and the city was baking in it. The air was thick and half the rain that fell sizzled into vapor the minute it hit pavement. Smart money was laying low and cool, only coming out after the sun had moved past the skyline and the night breeze had kicked up a little. I'd wandered my way to Duchess' offices — she was down at the Pooks building then, not her current digs — mainly because I was bored and annoying her was one of the sure-fire ways to not be bored.

She wasn't having any of it, though.

***

"I TOLD YOU, I'm not interested."

"Aw, come on, doll."

Green eyes slitted in a look that would scare a younger dog than me. "What did I say would happen next time you called me that?"

"You'd hook a claw into my nose and pull my spleen out through my nostril, yeah, yeah. Come on, it's be..." I had to pause, because 'fun' wasn't the word I was looking for, and neither was 'exciting.' "It'll be different!"

"It'll be nine hundred degrees on the pavement."

"We'll be on grass."

Whiskers twitched, unimpressed. "I hate grass."

"Okay, fine." I flopped down on the floor and stared up at where she was curled on the sofa, tail to nose, looking exactly like you'd expect a puss to look like on day five of a heat wave. The tile was cooler than the upholstery, but it didn't make me feel better. "Not like the bands were going to be any good, anyway. And the beer's always overpriced."

"And undrinkable. You hate music festivals. You hate crowds, period, especially if you're not being paid to patrol them. What do you really want?"

Busted. "I'm bored."

"Retirement must suck, huh?" The difference between sympathy and mockery is a cat's claw-tip.

"At least the station had air conditioning, even if it conked out half the summer."

"And made like a meat locker the other half."

"Yeah. And no, retirement doesn't suck. It's just too hot to do anything productive. So I figured I'd harass you, instead. Since you weren't exactly being a productive member of society when I got here."

She'd been playing solitaire, in point of fact. So that pretty much killed the conversation for a while, until we heard the whir-clunk-clunk of the elevator opening up on her floor.

Since there were only three offices currently in use, it seemed a decent bet that whoever it was coming up was maybe coming to see her. I scraped myself off the tile and tried to make my fur look presentable — probably a lost cause — but Duchess just uncurled her tail from over her nose, and lifted her head when there was a scratching noise outside her office door.

"Be a good dog and let them in on your way out?"

"You sure? I can—" I opened the door, and stopped when no potential client met my gaze. "Must've been a wrong number," I called over my shoulder, only to hear a faint cough somewhere around my paws.

I looked down.

"Oh. Hey. You got a lizard."

---

I WASN'T GOING ANYWHERE after that, and Duchess didn't even try to evict me. The lizard strutted in like he owned the place, and accepted a helping paw to the edge of the desk like Miss Universe ascending her throne.

"I want to hire you." His voice wasn't the squeak I'd expected, but a low, gravely rasp.

"I assumed you weren't here to sell me a bible," Duchess said, settling into her chair behind the desk and propping her chin on her paws. Her whiskers curled outward in attention, waiting for him to go on. I settled on one of the side chairs, and kept my trap shut. I'd never really thought about lizards before. Not exactly the sort of fellow you meet in the Alley, or elsewhere in the city for that matter, where rats and cockroaches are more likely to be scuttling along the brickwork. But we had enough green spaces and sunny perches, I suppose there had to be some, somewhere.

He wasn't hard to look at, either; sort of shimmery along his backside, from flat head to elongated tail, greenish-purple skin that looked to shade to orange along the belly, not that I was going to be rude enough to ask to see.

"Your name?" Duchess prompted.

"Scada. My name is Scada." The lizard's eyes rolled to her, then me, as though expecting us to react. "I need you to find my hoard."

"I...beg your pardon?"

"My hoard." Scada quivered in indignation, from the back of his neck to the tip of his tail. "Someone stole my hoard!"

---

So YEAH, that's where we ended up, late on a Tuesday night. Taking notes on the alleged theft of a lizard's hoard. If it weren't for the twitching of Duchess' whiskers, and the way one ear kept pinning back, you'd swear she was taking this serious as taxes. I — not being the private investigator currently under hire — had no such compulsions. But if I snarked at the client, she'd kick me out, possibly not bothering to use the door, and I had to see how this played out.

---

"I can't believe you talked me into coming with me."

"I can't believe I agreed to do this for free." My usual's five solid per day, plus expenses, which is even more than Duchess charges for anything except abduction cases. And yet here I was creeping along behind her because a purplish-green lizard claimed his hoard had been stolen, like some kind of miniature dragon with a pocketful of small change and sequins.

But I figured it would make for a good story, being firsthand when the great Duchess bursts in on another lizard and steals back...well, a handful of change and some sequins.

The story was, Scada — henceforth referred to as The Client — had been minding his own business, when an older lizard had come in and taken everything while he was on a bug-and-brew break. He'd seen the tail heading out the door with the last of all his worldly belongings and—he claimed — had known who it was immediately. Maybe. He thought.

It was easy money, since Scada knew who and where. All we had to do was go collect it. Duchess didn't ask him why he didn't go to the cops with this; the lizard was shift-eyed enough to suggest that maybe not all the 'hoard' had been gotten free and clean in the first place. The thought of there being a chain of little lizard heists happening all around us was probably what had possessed me to come along. The great Duchess, scooping coins into her pocket and hotfooting out of some tiled hole in the wall? I had to be there for that.

---

THE ADDRESS the client had given us was a reasonably decent location, a two-up two-down apartment building with a brick facade and insides that wouldn't send a health inspector or a fire safety warden running for their citation book. But that's about all that could be said for it. The lights in the foyer and staircase were enough to see by, but dim enough to hide the fact that nothing had been painted in the past decade, and the carpet underneath was clean, but threadbare.

Cheap housing, but not a slumlord. Not where it was visible, anyway.

Our destination was on the second floor, apartment C. We didn't bother being stealthy. Duchess knocked once on the door, then tested the handle.

It was open.

She flicked an ear at me . I shrugged. This was her show. She wanted to bust in without an invite, that was up to her.

Me, I wouldn't have bothered knocking, but I've got a badge to back me up. And most people never bother to look at the tiny print that says "retired."

"Hello? Any—"

I've never seen her move that fast, not even the time the water main burst. But instead of water this time, she was dancing back on all fours from — flame?

I tensed, but it flickered and died out, leaving the air tinged with smoke, like someone had been using the tiniest flame-thrower.

Duchess' eyes were all pupil when she looked at me, her tail fluffed and her whiskers plastered to her face, and if I hadn't been just as shocked, I probably would have laughed.

"Hello?"

Another gust of flame came out, but this time it was aimed at the wall next to the door, not us. Either that, or whoever was holding the flamethrower had crappy aim.

"Cut that out!" Duchess snapped.

There was a noise, like a choked sob, and then silence. But nothing flamed-on.

Duchess gave me another glance, then poked her whiskers back through the door. "We're going to come in, okay? Stop with the attempted barbecue."

There was no response, then the scratching of claws on hardwood. "Not like there's anything left for you to steal anyway" a petulant voice muttered. "Come in, take the damned toilet paper and my mac and cheese, that's abut all I have left, fucking sorry state of affairs, this fucking world I swear, a drake can't cut a break, their own home isn't safe and then they get *yelled* at..."

The door led into a large room, currently decorated with a sofa, and a rug, and that was it. Well, and a lizard, square in the middle of the rug, glaring at us like we were responsible for everything shitty that had ever happened to him.

"You Balthy?"

"Balthazar, yes, and who the hell is asking, fur-face?"

"My name's Duchess." She didn't drag me into the introductions, which I appreciated. "I'm here to the back a few items you seem to have misappropriated."

I'd never heard a lizard laugh before. Of course, before this, I'd never seen one cry before, either. Balthy — Balthazar — managed to do both.

"Do I like like I've got someone else's hoard?" he asked us, finally. "You're about three hours too late, furry. I got cleaned out. Everything, gone. Unless you want the mac and cheese. Not like I've got an appetite right now, anyway."

Well. That was... not expected. I sat down and started cleaning a paw, waiting for Duchess to pull her next move.

"No, you keep it," she said, sitting down on her haunches, and then sliding onto the floor gracefully, so her nose was level with the lizard's eyes. I tensed. It blinked once at her in surprise, but didn't drop any more heat.

"Let me get this down," she said. "You stole from Scada —"

"Who?"

"My client. Greenish-purple?"

"Yeah, maybe."

"You stole from him, and someone else stole from you?"

"Oh good, logic is in your skill sets. Duh."

"What was stolen?"

"Everything!" Flames exploded around the words, making Duchess scramble backward on the rug, all presence at grace forgotten, trying to avoid the blast of heat.

The lizard snapped its mouth shut, looked mournfully at the tip of its snout, and turned tail, marching squarely across the rug to another door, which it flung open and then slammed shut behind.

Duchess stared at the door, then twisted around to stare at the charred wall by the door, and let out a little huff of surprise. "Well. Never saw that before."

Neither had I but I wasn't going to admit that. "Not like we know many lizards."

"Maybe we should work on that."

I ear-twitched my opinion of that. Fire-spitters or no, Balthy still looked like something I'd set a pup to play with before dinner, not talk to.

<hr>

"Balthazar?"

"No."

"Balthy, tell us who took your stuff."

There was the sound of movement on the other side of the door. "I don't know."

"I think you do."

Listening to Duchess, you'd think she knew every impure thought you'd ever had in your life. Only the twitch of her tail gave her away. The tail always gives it away, for a puss. They just can't control that last inch.

I might have an advantage, though, not having much of a tail to speak of.

There was a muttered noise from behind the door, and Duchess' ears twitted forward sharply. Her tail stilled, then I could see her entire body tense, just a bit. She had a lead.

"No," she said, although it sounded more like agreement than refusal. "We won't come back."

———

THE AIR OUTSIDE was still too warm, despite the sun going down, but I'd promised to stick with her on this, and by now I was seriously curious to see where we'd end up.

"You got a name?"

"No name. But a location." Her whiskers didn't seem pleased by it, though. "You might want to step down from this one, Buddy. I get the feeling he was sending me there to get rid of me, if you know what I mean."

"Puss. You really think, even if I were still bored — which I'm not, for the record, I'd dump you after a crap thing like that?" I put a paw to my chest. "Please. I am insulted. Hurt that you should think such a thing of me. Nay, offended, even."

Her whiskers eased a little, and she snorted. "Come on, then."

———

THE LOCATION she'd been given was uptown, financially if not physically. There's not much that's uptown about the Alley. But the building we arrived at had a well-maintained facade of brick and dark blue trim around the door, and no windows for the first three floors, then ringed around with some seriously impressive viewports on the fourth.

They used to build 'em like this back when the Alley was more of a back alley. And nothing good happened in 'em.

The door was open, like the other one, but it had less a sense of forgetfulness or neglect than invitation.

The kind of invitation a spider leaves.

"I've got a bad feeling about this."

"Shut up," Duchess muttered, but her whiskers were quivering, and her ears were pulled back like she was readying herself for a fight. Her tail wasn't twitching: worse, it was straight out behind her, stiffly quivering.

The first floor was entirely open space. And I mean, open space: no walls, no furniture, no nothing except a staircase. All right, then. For the first time, I regretted no longer carrying regularly.

"Formation," I said, and it wasn't a suggestion. Duchess glared, but dropped back to let me take lead. It wasn't machismo or speciesism: I was bulkier.

The second floor had a kitchen layout. Nice, too. Someone had spent some money on it.

"Third floor bedroom?"

"Or a really luxe bathroom."

We were talking low, the voices they teach you when a whisper's gonna carry and alert your prey. But we went up the next flight, anyway.

It wasn't a bedroom. Or a bathroom. It was the two-story atrium of the world's most bedazzled hoarder.

"Sweet mother of milk," Duchess breathed, peering over my shoulder, and there was nothing I could add to that. There had to be a million coins gathered on the floor, maybe a million and two, and it was all covered in shiny, from bedraggled tinsel clearly yanked off someone's dying Christmas tree to what I couldn't swear but would totally swear were the glint of diamond rings.

"And this guy felt the need to snatch from poor schmucks like Scada and Balthy?"

I was about to snark back at her, when we both realized that the pile wasn't just coins and glitter.

The triangular head turned, the neck uncurling, and I was pretty sure I heard my stomach drop to somewhere around my paws.

"We grow with our hoards. Everyone knows that."

The voice was cool and whispery, and the narrow tongue that flickered at us, clearly getting more information about its unexpected visitors, wasn't in the least bit reassuring. It may not have had visible teeth in that narrow slit of a mouth, but the claws that scrabbled over the hoard as it came over to face us were larger and nastier-looking than anything Duchess was carrying, and it probably outweighed me by twice again, based on the ripple of muscle under the scales.

"If we don't grow our hoard, we don't grow. We don't grow... well, we're at risk. This is a big bad city, you've got to be big and bad to live in it."

"Right." I'll give Duchess credit: her voice was cool, nonchalant as if they'd met sipping martinis at some fancy social invite-only event. Or what I imagined shit like that would go down, not having ever gotten an invite myself. She slipped past me, her tail flicking me on the nose as she went past. Right. I was to sit back and be muscle if needed. I wasn't sure how much help I'd be if this one spat fire, too; it was easily four times the size of poor Balthy and I got the feeling its flame-thrower would be larger, too. I mean, I could take it, if I needed to. But it wouldn't be easy, and I'd be stuck growing out singed fur for at least a week.

"But once you've grown, you don't go back, right?" Duchess was moving slow and easy, keeping out what I guess she thought was the lizard's lunge-range. "So you won't mind if I reclaim what you took from my client, since it's—"

The warning gust of flame suggested that this particular lizard minded very much.

"What's mine is mine."

"Yeah well, it wasn't yours to take?"

Steam lifted from the pinprick nostrils, and I shifted and grumbled — okay, growled, maybe — until that triangular head tilted to look past her at me. I showed my canines and deepened my chest, settling into the very best rendition of "serve and protect and will not move" the academy ever taught. It was probably more impressive when I was five years younger and more muscle, but it still looked pretty good, if I do say so as shouldn't.

"It's mine now. That's how the world works."

Scales wasn't wrong, and Duchess knew it. That didn't mean she wasn't going to try, though. Not because she believed in fair play or good will toward all, specifically, but she'd taken on a client, and she was going to do her damnedest to come through. I'd known her since she was a kit, and that was just how she walked.

"We could bargain for it? Maybe a few rounds of riddles...?"

The next blast of fire was stronger, and nearly reached her, even jumping back a step.

"Riddles bore me, and games of chance are for idiots. I take what I want and I keep what I take." The slitted eyes opened wider, then closed again. "Be thankful I see nothing on you I wish to take."

And that was our cue to get out of here. I braced myself to

haul her back down the steps by force and by the scruff if needed.

"All right," Duchess said, possibly surprising both me and the lizard. "Keep what you've taken. But you won't be able to take any more."

"You are threatening me, fur-skin?" The steam thickened menacingly.

"Not at all. Merely stating a fact. You're big, and you're reasonably scary, but you're not the biggest and you're not the scariest, and for every fire there's a firefighter, if you know what I mean."

Her ears were erect and her tail was proud, and I totally believed her for about eleven seconds. At which point we were on the stairs heading down and every muscle in her body was trembling so hard I ended up having to carry her out after all.

Not by the scruff, though. She'd earned that much dignity.

---

"I think he believed you," I said, one we were out on the street. Wonders of wonders the air felt cooler in comparison.

"He didn't believe me," she corrected me, and checked her phone, then started down the street with the air of a puss on a mission, making me trot to keep up. "But he had a second of doubt settle into his gut, and that's almost as good."

"Huh." I didn't see it, but Duchess is smarter than me in some ways, so I let it go. Then; "hey, where're we going? This isn't the way back—"

"I got a couple of errands to run, first."

It wasn't like I had anywhere else to go, so I tagged along. I wasn't looking forward to going back and admitting to her client that we hadn't gotten his hoard back, either. And maybe the stores would have decent air conditioning, or we could stop for coffee.

Our first stop ending up being the local bank. I knew the security guard, a Pinscher who'd taken his five-and-done from the force and turned it into a steady gig eyeballing shoppers. We nodded to each other, the way you do, and I watched while Duchess waited in line to hand over a couple of twenties for a bag of rolled coins.

"You need to do a shit-ton of laundry?"

"Shut up and be useful," she said, shoving the bag at me until I took it. It was heavier than it looked; she might've handed over a fifty, not a twenty.

"We done? I'd kill for coffee."

"One more stop." She paused in the foyer and consulted her phone, then nodded once and headed off down a side street. It wasn't the worst neighborhood I'd ever been in, not by a long shot, but I had no idea what she was up to, or if there was a coffee shop nearby I'd trust my tastebuds in.

Duchess stopped in front of a dinky little storefront, and disappeared through a door with a swear-to-god tinkly bell over it. The nostalgia factor alone dragged me in after her.

I almost backed out again: the store was crammed full of huge rolls of fabric and shelves of plastic bins filled with enough gewgaws and fiddly bits to ... I have no idea what people did with them, actually.

Duchess looked as lost as I was, until a clerk wandered over and they had a quick huddle before scooping up a handful here and a handful there, until they'd collected another couple of twenties' worth of sequins and rhinestones, the gaudiest godawful things I'd ever seen.

By now I'd figured out what she was doing, but I needed confirmation.

"Seriously?" I asked, as the clerk stuffed it all into plastic bags with the store's logo on them. "You're buying it a new hoard?"

Her whiskers twitched, and she gave me a sideways, scornful look. "I said I'd get him his hoard back. I didn't say it was going to be the exact same one. And if Scada's going to grow, I want it to grow thinking kindly of me."

---

"So yeah. that's the story of Duchess got the favor of a fire-breathing lizard."

There was a snort of amusement from the other end of the table "And how Uncle Buddy learned how to BeDazzle."

"We are never speaking of that again. Ever."

Or at least, not unless someone refills my glass, toot suite.

# THE CASE OF THE SEASIDE SWINDLE

I was staring out the window, my whiskers twitching at the unfamiliar and unwanted smells and sounds, when someone came up beside me and coughed, then waited.

"I don't take vacation. I don't need vacation."

The conductor taking my ticket wasn't any more impressed than Sparks had been when he put me on the train twenty minutes ago, still protesting. He snapped a hole in the slip of paper and tucked it into the metal clip over my seat, and moved on, tail twitching idly in boredom.

I went back to staring out the window. It was two hours and twenty-seven minutes to my destination, but I couldn't tell you what we passed, or what any of it looked like, other than bleak, and cold. And flat. How the hell was anything that flat?

"I really don't need a vacation," I told the cabbie who threw my suitcase into the back of his car, and held the door so I could get in.

"Picked a nice place to not vacation," he said, with the sarcasm only ear-bit rabbits can manage, then leadfooted out of the train stop's parking lot like a fox was on his tail.

I wasn't sulking. I was irritated at being bullied into leaving town, that was it.

My office — the entire building — was being fumigated. They did it every three years if we needed it or not, and honestly it needed it every year, if not more often. Normally I'd just work from home for the three days it took for the air to be breathable again. But we'd had a cold front move in, which meant my apartment went from being a cozy little den to an ice cube, because my landlord was a cheap-ass rat.

And bad luck compounding with bad luck, just around then Sparks showed up on my doorstop to inform me that a particular rat-eater had been released on parole, and I might want to make myself scarce for a few days until he inevitably did something that got him thrown back into the kennel.

Since the rat-eater and I have a bit of an unpleasant history, the warning made sense. I could have gotten a room in a hotel somewhere in town, holed up and caught up on my Netflix backlog. That would have been the plan, if Sparks hadn't then mentioned, so casually, that he had a friend who had a little place down the shore, empty this week, and maybe I'd like to spend a few days listening to the ocean and chilling. Cheaper than a hotel. Take a nice vacation.

I hate the ocean. I hate sand. And I don't take vacations.

"Welcome to Point Promise. Enjoy your vacation, ma'am."

---

THE KEY TO THE HOUSE — cottage, really — was taped under the eaves where any marauding squirrel could have laid claws on it, but hey, I don't judge. Much. I dropped my bag in the foyer and took a look around. Clean, which was a relief, and definitely seaside-tacky, with the floral print upholstery on the sofa and armchairs, and seashell decor everything else, but nothing that made me want to turn around and check into a Motel 9. The kitchen was sparse but equally clean, with both basic cooking supplies and a folder filled with take-out menus on the two-person table, next to a list of emergency phone numbers.

So far, not too horrible.

The second floor was three bedrooms, each barely large enough to fit a double bed, and a single bathroom. From the window of the bathroom I could see over the tops of the houses next door to where the pale blue of the ocean stretched out into the horizon. Two blocks away, I remembered Sparks telling me.

Stupid dog. He probably enjoyed chasing waves and getting salt in his fur.

I went back downstairs, grabbed my bag, and dropped it in the largest of the small bedrooms, the one with the window facing the front street. Then, ignoring the no doubt delightful lures of a closed-for-off-season downtown or a cold and windy beach, I curled up on the surprisingly comfortable bed, and took a nap.

Don't judge. I was on vacation.

---

In new places, one ear always stayed cocked, no matter how sweet the nap, so when I heard a noise downstairs, my eyes opened immediately, and my whiskers twitched, trying to determine where the threat was coming from. It took a second or three before I identified the noise as a doorbell. Specifically, the doorbell of the door downstairs.

Someone was at the door.

I considered ignoring it: I hadn't called for delivery, and Sparks was the only one who knew where I was, and if he needed to tell me something he'd call, not show up on my doorstep. Probably some inane edition of the welcome wagon, or someone trying to convince me to save my ninth life for god, or something.

I closed my eyes and rearranged my paws over my nose.

Then the buzzer rang again, and there was something about the way they leaned on the buzzer than had me heading downstairs before I'd even decided to get out of bed.

Desperation, I decided, as I padded to the entrance. That weight was desperation. Which was enough to make me pause and check for anything that could be used as a weapon — a shell-encrusted ceramic vase within reach, check — before I unlatched and opened the door.

On the other side of the door was a kit, barely old enough to be out on his own, grey fur dripping wet with — from the smell — a full-body dip in the ocean that they didn't seem to have enjoyed.

"Miss? Miss you're the only one home I've rung all the doorbells do you have a phone?"

I did a quick once-over and didn't see any blood or obvious bones. "Are you hurt, is anyone else hurt?" I've learned to get the important questions out of the way first, while they're still talking, before shock or protective ignorance shuts their mouths again.

"I'm fine, I got hit by a wave," and he shook himself, sending droplets flying, as though to prove his able-bodiedness, "but miss, we need to call the police. There's a body on the beach."

<hr>

Sparks likes to say I've become a smidge cynical with adulthood, but he's lying: I was cynical straight out of weaning. So rather than dial 9-1-1 immediately, I grabbed my coat and my phone, threw a dry towel over the kit, and told him to take me to where he'd seen the body.

It wasn't that I didn't trust the kit, I just like to check things out myself before I involve the cops.

It was two blocks to the boardwalk, streets flat as a Monopoly board and about as excitingly laid out. We crossed the road and went up the wooden stairs over the seawall, then down even more rickety stairs to the sand itself. As expected, the sand crunched unpleasantly under-paw, and I hated it immediately. The ocean was a muted roar in the background, the wind thankfully dying down, so at least we weren't blinded by flying sand. Small blessings.

"Over there," the kit pointed. "It was right — "

His voice dropped off, and his ears flattened, either in shock or anger.

There was nothing there, just a sweep of grayish-white sand.

"It was there! Miss, I swear to you, I was walking along the beach, and I saw it, and I was so shocked that's when the wave caught me, and it was there! It was right there!"

The kit was hysterical, the kind that would earn an Emmy if it was acting, so I took a minute to scruff him until he calmed down.

Big, watery eyes turned up at me, pitiful enough to melt brick. "Miss, I swear."

"I believe you." I did. I was a pretty good judge of liars, and this kit wasn't one, yet. But that didn't mean someone else hadn't been punking *him*. Town like this, winter probably got boring as piss. Scaring your friends — or better yet, total strangers — would be a nice break. Not that I'd ever done anything like that myself. "Stay here," and then I checked myself. "No, go up there," and I pointed at the mild shelter the boardwalk pilings provided, "and stay warm. I'll go check it out."

Normally I'd keep a witness close, but the kit was still shivering, despite the towel. I wouldn't get anything out of him if he went down with pneumonia. He took off without argument, stopped when he reached the windbreak, and turned around to watch, to make sure I'd do what I'd said I would.

I made sure he was staying put, then took a careful look around. There wasn't anyone else on the beach near us, although there were figures walking along the boardwalk, heads down and shoulders hunched walking like their sole purpose in life was to be somewhere else five minutes ago. I circled around where the kit said the body had been, moving closer cautiously, scanning the sand in front of me for anything that might look...

I had no idea what I was looking for, what kind of evidence might be left behind. I had no idea what sand should look like, either on a perfectly calm summer day or in midwinter bluster. I knew that it felt weirdly hard under my pads, dry granules scattering over my fur as I moved. I didn't like it as much as I'd thought I wouldn't like it. There were bits of dried sticks and cracked pieces of shell scattered in the sand, and the occasional scratchy marks of bird-toes, moving around discarded bits of trash half-buried and abandoned, but that was it. Nothing that said, "there had been a body here."

But...

I lifted my head to look around again, even as I felt my claws flex, digging into the sand like I was preparing to leap on something. The old hunting instinct isn't as buried as civilized folk like to think, and a smart puss learns to listen to it when it growls. But what had set it off?

I made another circle, moving closer to the water despite every other instinct telling me to get away from it. I'm not one of those pusses who enjoys getting splashed, so sue me. But there was something that caught my attention. Not the waves themselves, but the sand closer, where it was damp...

There. Faint, and only visible because the sand was wet and heavy, keeping it from blowing away and erasing the marks. I kept one eye on the water, ready to back up if a wave came further up the beach than expected, and crouched to investigate. There were definite marks there, not straight but slightly wiggly, and I quickly found a matching set, the sand between them pressed down a claw's depth, as though something heavy — maybe about the size and weight of a poodle — had been dragged. I stood up and traced the lines back to where the kit claimed to have seen the body, disappearing as the sand dried, then turned back to follow the lines until they disappeared.

Into the ocean.

Bracing myself, I stepped closer, wincing as the cold salt water touched my paws, and tried to see into the greenish-blue water. Tiny fish flicked back and forth, then disappeared, spooked by my shadow, but there was nothing else except cracked shells and drifts of seaweed.

If there had been a body — or *something* — there, it was gone now.

But there was no indication of anything else around it. I checked, twice. No footprints, no conveniently-identifying debris. Nothing except the heavy lines of a body being dragged and disappearing.

Well, shit. I could feel my whiskers curling in anticipation.

Looks like there was a case here after all.

---

THE TIDE WAS COMING in around my paws; based on the line between damp sand and dry, this area would be under water again pretty soon. I took a handful of photos of the sand with my phone, but I didn't think they were going to help.

Whoever it was who'd gotten offed, they'd either died of natural causes and a scavenger hauled them into the water for consumption, or they'd been killed and the body disposed of, probably via water-based scavenger.

Either way, I definitely wasn't going swimming any time soon.

I trudged back to the dock where the kit was waiting, watching me with pupils still too wide for daylight, although he'd dried off and calmed down, the towel abandoned on the sand behind him.

"Well?"

"All right, um... what the hell's your name, anyway?"

"Siddig."

"All right, Siddig. It's okay, I believe you."

Siding's eats went flat and his tail dropped and quivered, pathetically thankful as I told him that yes, something had been there; probably a body; yes, I believed him; and yeah, I'd take over from here. Some kits want to be involved in trouble up to their whiskers; it was nice to see one willing to wait at least until full growth before tossing their first life into the shitter.

Siddig seemed perfectly willing to leave this entire shit show to the adults.

I watched him lope off to wherever home was, part of me wishing I had that option. This wasn't a job, I wasn't getting paid for this, I should hand it over to someone who *was*. But unlike the Alley, I had no contacts in this town, no backup with the local woofers, and I was pretty damn sure they wouldn't take kindly to some Alley PI showing up and telling them there'd been a probably dead body dragged off into the surf, based on the eyewitness evidence of a half-grown kit and some sand markings that were going to be gone by the time I got anyone to listen to me.

It would get filed as a crank report, and nothing would get done.

Hell, for all I knew, it was a crank report. Yeah, there'd been a body. Yeah, it had been dragged. Yeah... but.

But.

If I'd even had half the brain I'd been accused of having, I'd go back to the cottage, find something boring to read, and spend the next few days napping until it was safe for me to go home. This wasn't my issue, and it wasn't like Siddig was ever going to know I'd lied to him.

And it wasn't actually, technically a lie. I'd said I'd take over, I'd never said I'd look into it. I'd certainly never said I'd investigate. The kit didn't even *know* that's what I did for a living. I was just some adult they'd dumped this on, so they didn't have to worry about it any longer.

Sweet cream and cupcakes, I was the adult in this scenario. That's make a lot of pusses laugh.

Still. Technically, I had done everything I'd promised to, already.

I managed to buy that for about three steps and realized that technicalities were shit lawyers argued over. I'd given that kit the impression that I was going to find out what happened to the body, and yeah, there was wiggle room and he'd never know... but I would.

And then there was the fact that I was one of those kits who was always in trouble up to their whiskers. No reason to think it was going to change now.

With a sigh, I walked back to the cottage, trying to figure out what my next move would be. I was almost to the porch, key in my paw, when inspiration, of a sort, hit me.

When in doubt, the old cop who'd not-so-gently steered me

into my current profession used to say, "stop by your local and have a beer while you think about it."

All right, he'd actually said coffee, but the premise was the same. Don't rush into anything; stop and think. And, more to the point, do it somewhere someone might be able to drop inspiration on you.

It was still early in the afternoon, but the bar I'd spotted when we crossed the boardwalk had a faintly-blinking 'open' sign in the window, and there were cars in the narrow parking lot, so I turned around and headed there. If nothing else, it was always useful to know the nearest watering hole. Even if I didn't intend to stay past the time it would take to clean out my office and for the rat-eater to get caught doing something that revoked his bail. Three days should about do it, knowing all the players...

The bar didn't look like much from the outside, and looked like even less from the inside, but the scuffled wooden floor was clean, and the bar had the minimum essentials of two old men scowling into their beer and a bored-looking bartender at the other end, polishing glasses to keep busy, so it suited my needs.

"Hey." I dropped into the stool halfway down the bar, resting my elbows in a calculated slouch. One of the old men looked up at me, long nose twitching, then went back to his more interesting beer. The other one didn't even flick an ear.

The bartender was a fox, and I mean that both ways. Unusual, but considering some of the servers I'd seen over the years in the Alley, not anything I was going to complain about.

"What can I do ya for?"

I gave the taps a long once-over. "Stout, please." Nothing fancy, but nothing that would make him dismiss me, either. There's a trick to working bartenders, and generally they're full-aware you're doing it, so you can't afford to screw up.

The stout was room temperature, and deeply satisfying. It'll kill me someday, I'm told, but the indulgence is worth it. "I'm

Duchy," I said, sliding my ten across the bar and leaving it there. Could be paying for the beer, could be opening a tab. So long as he didn't touch it, I had an opening.

"Good name," he said, but didn't offer his own. Fair enough: I hadn't given him my real name, anyway.

I gave an ostentatious once-over around the space. "So. This the normal excitement around town?"

Fox whiskers aren't as expressive as a puss', but he did a pretty good job of conveying politely-faked interest. "Cold weather slows things down a bit. We get enough excitement once it warms up."

"I can imagine. Boardwalk must bring all the fake IDs out."

That got me a sharp-toothed grin, brief but real. Bingo. "Not too bad in here," he said. "We've a zero-tolerance policy, and every three-four we send on a long trip off a short pier, to teach 'em a lesson."

I thought of the water that had nipped at my heels and shuddered. Going full-in, especially at night, was nothing I wanted to imagine. "Bet they don't try that twice."

"College students," and the words were laced with a mix of disgust and pride. "Some of 'em, it takes three tries to get through."

I snorted in appreciation, and took another sip of the stout while he went down to the far end of the bar to check on his old men. They didn't need to talk, just pushed their glasses toward him for a refill.

I waited.

A few minutes later, he glided back to position across the bar from me, and I bit back a smile. Gotcha.

"So, what's it like here in the summer? I came down for a little quiet, but I'm thinking too much quiet goes a long way toward terminal boredom."

"Teenagers, drunks, tourists, and teenaged drunk tourists."

He shrugged and started polishing another glass. "They're not that bad, though. Steady money, and no real troublemakers. Mostly, those go down the road a bit. We get more families around here, some of 'em've been here long enough the kids go from playing the games to running 'em. Half the staff here in the summer used to get kicked out for trying to sneak in, underage."

"Train 'em early, huh?" I revised my opinion; this wasn't a bartender; this was the owner. Or manager, at least.

"Only way to be sure."

"So busy in the summer, but you know everyone in town, off-season?"

"Name, rank, and what time they go to bed. And sometimes, with whom."

One of the old men let out a creaking laugh at that, letting me know that sound carried down the bar. Or, he'd just thought of something particularly rudely funny, and it had nothing to do with this conversation.

"Nice," I said to my new friend. "My neck of the woods, nobody'd notice if I went AWOL until my rent was twenty minutes overdue. Bet around here, a guy takes a powder, the gossip's round town in ten."

"Seven, if he took a powder with someone else." My host was settling into storytelling mode, bracing his hip against the bar. "Last time it happened, two boys upped and off with each other, everyone knew before the girlfriend left behind was crying on a new boy's shoulder."

For a PI that kind of gossip-line was a dream come true, but personally it made my tail twitch with anxiety. I preferred my traumas to not be community theater, if I could avoid it, and most folk I knew felt the same. I guess that's why we stay in the Alley, rather than ending up here.

But this wasn't about me. It was about that dead body on the beach, and the kit I'd made a promise to. "So nothing exciting this winter, huh?"

"Boring as an oatmeal shit."

So that was that. Two hours, a little cross-species flirting we both knew wasn't going anywhere, and another stout and shot later, I headed back to my little cottage.

Night came quick out here, without the lights of the Alley overhead, and the darkening air made the sound of the ocean seem both closer and louder. I might have started walking a little faster than usual, just to put that noise a little farther behind me.

Not that I had any paranoid delusions of the ocean as some-thing that could flow up over the beach and pull me down into it... but then again, *something* had done just that.

I could check with the cops, but I didn't think I'd get a different official answer than what Jock told me; nobody's gone missing from town in the past month, and any gossip from nearby towns made its way through Point Promise nearly as fast.

Whoever the body on the beach had been, they'd either been an outsider, or they'd just died that afternoon. Or both.

If I were smart, I'd decide this was as far as I could go, particularly since I wasn't getting paid. I'd gone as far as a promise required me to go. But I was curious, now.

And I still had a couple of lives left to spend on it.

So, despite my desire to get as far away from that echo of the waves as possible, I turned around and headed into town proper, where the brighter lights, such as they were, promised warmth, food, and the possibility of more gossip.

* * *

JOEY'S ADVERTISED the finest pizza on or off the boardwalk, and also burgers, twice-cooked fries, and egg creams. They were doing better business than the bar, and all of the customers were well under the drinking age, except for a handful of adults huddled in a corner booth, poking intently at a blueprint of something, held down with what looked like milkshake glasses.

To my surprise, there was a human behind the counter.

"You're new," he said, sliding a menu across the counter.

"I'm getting that a lot," I said. I was feeling the shot a bit, so I opened with a burger, rare, and a coke, and the waiter nodded, yelling the order across the half-wall metal partition to where several bodies were moving in what looked like practiced precision.

"The double take gave you away," he admitted. "Point Promise's pretty mixed. All sorts end up here, and not all of us escape."

"Getting a lot of that, too. But it seems like a nice place?"

"Sure, except for the drunks, the rowdies, the druggies, and the dead bodies, it's a paradise."

My ears may have twitched a little too sharply at that, but I was pretty sure he missed it. Even when they're trying, they can't always read us very well.

"Dead bodies?" I kept my tone politely incredulous.

"Seaside town," he said with a shrug, grabbing my soda off the half-wall where it had been deposited, and dropping it next to me without spilling a drop, snatching a paper-wrapped straw along the way, seemingly from out of thin air. "You go out a bit on the water, even the fish can't catch everything that happens out there. A bad argument, a quiet splash, and hey, that spouse or business partner or unfortunate client... not a problem any more. It happens. Less now than it used to; I could tell you some stories about the bad old days. But it happens."

Bless humans and their fascination with all things gory. "And what happens to the bodies?"

My waiter shrugged, and over his shoulder, over the half wall, I saw pizza dough rise into the air almost casually caught expertly by black paws. So they weren't all human back there. Good to know.

"Sometimes, the cops haul 'em in. Sometimes the sharks get 'em. Sometimes the gulls and crabs do. All depends on who gets there first."

I stripped the paper off the straw, and took a long sip, contemplating the possibility that the body hadn't been dragged into the water, but up onto the beach. But that still didn't explain what had happened to it in the time between the kit seeing it, and my arrival on the scene. I was pretty sure crabs and gulls couldn't have picked a corpse clean that fast, not bones included.

And if a shark had gotten up into the sand and dragged a body back *into* the water, I was packing up and going back to the Alley *now*, because that's some bullshit I had not been informed about.

The burger landed before I could ask another question, and he disappeared to deal with someone who'd asked for their check. I took a few minutes to savor the burger; it wasn't the best I'd ever had, but it was juicy and thick, and they hadn't ruined it with ketchup, and some days that's all a carnivore needs.

By the time the counter guy came back, I was sopping up what was left of the juices with what was left of the fries, which were, as promised, crisp as an arson scene.

"For fries like this, I might be tempted to risk a few dead bodies," I admitted. "So long as they don't wash up on the beach like hypodermic needles, totally ruining the day." I left it not quite as a question, but with a faint uptick at the end, as though inviting him to reassure me.

He gave me an odd once-and-over, then just shook his head and then put down my check and turned away, the set of his shoulders telling me we were done. I blinked, not sure what I'd done to shut him down.

"You keep that pretty pink nose of yours clean, you should be fine," a voice said to my left.

I kept my ears and tail still and tilted my head to see who was talking to me. He was a heavy-set Boxer, scattering of white on his snout and a nasty scar over one eye that looked like it had been cut with a jagged bottle-edge and stitched with something as nasty.

Whoever he was, I didn't like him. Not the least of which because he'd chased off my informant.

I flattened my ears just a bit more than was polite and widened my eyes at him. "Excuse me?"

The Boxer wasn't buying. "You're a sharp puss, you heard what I said. Iff'n you're as sharp as you look, you'll listen, too."

Those kinds of compliments were the kind that weren't. It was hardly the first time I'd been told to take my whiskers out of something, but usually I know who's telling me. And never once has it actually worked.

"That all depends on if I think I'm hearing anything with listening to. What's your name, good-looking?"

The sarcasm didn't even make a dent in his plush coat. "Buster."

Suuuure it was. In certain circles of which I was glancingly acquainted, 'buster' was what you called an errand-boy of certain stature, the one trusted with setting up meets that might lead to treaties — or ambushes. I didn't think I'd been in town long enough to warrant either, even if I had been poking my whiskers too deep into someone else's bowl, but small towns could be weird.

But had talking about dead bodies in general gotten me this welcoming committee, or was it a singular body in particular?

My whiskers twitched. "And if I keep my nose clean, as you suggest?"

"Point Promise can be a lovely place to spend some downtime," he said, as though agreeing to something I'd suggested. He picked up my still-untouched check, and laid down a twenty in its place, then slid his wide backside off the stool and trudged with studied deliberateness toward a back table, set at just the right angle that I couldn't see who, if anyone, was sitting there.

I wasn't sure if I'd just been warned off or baited into looking deeper. Probably, both. Somewhere, back in the Alley, Captain Sparks just facepawed himself, and didn't know why.

THAT'S TOTALLY A LIE. He'd know why.

---

THIS WASN'T THE ALLEY, and I hadn't brought clothing appropriate for skulking around the beach after dark, so after Buster made his exit, I did too.

The night air had gotten sharply colder, or maybe the restaurant had been warmer than I'd realized. Nobody followed me back to the cottage, not unless they were a hell of a lot better than they should be in a podunk beach town in off-season, and warnings and dead bodies aside, I really didn't think they would be.

The question of *why* I'd just gotten warned off lingered, but there wasn't anything I could do just then except go to sleep and hope that my hindbrain figured something out for me by morning.

The bed was as comfortable as I'd remembered from my nap, what seemed like days and days ago, and my ears had barely hit the pillow before I was out. What seemed like minutes later, I determined the error I'd made in choosing this bedroom: the morning sunlight came straight in the window. That might be a plus for morning pusses, but even after going to sleep stupid early the night before, I wasn't prepared to be conscious that close to dawn.

My sleep had been dreamless, as far as I could recall, and left me without any new ideas of what might be going on, or why Buster had been sent to give me that message. I lay on my side, a leg over my eyes to block the sun, and considered that whoever owned the house might have mentioned that a PI was staying there, and that had been a general polite warning from the local crime syndicate.

It seemed as reasonable an explanation as any, and I'd found over the years that the reasonable one, especially when it came to professional crime, was usually the true one.

Still, I was up. And short of curling on the seashell-uphol-stered sofa and reading a tatty paperback all day, I might as well go see if the alleged crime scene gave up anything more under direct daylight.

---

THE SKY WAS BLUE, the sun was out, but it was still too cold out on the beach for my idea of fun. Nonetheless, there was a young family spread out on a plaid blanket, the parents huddled over a thermos of what I was going to assume was coffee, while their three pups scattered sand and dared each other to get their paws wet in the wavelets before dashing back with alarmed barks when the water actually reached them.

The water was silver-blue where the sun hit it, shading to a darker color under the clouds, and while I still had no desire to get close, I could appreciate the roughness of it. It was a lot like the Alley, in some ways; sometimes calm, sometimes stormy, but a hell of a lot deeper and more dangerous than the surface would suggest.

I wasn't sure what that made the fools out there on surf-boards, other than, well, fools.

From where I'd stopped by the wooden pillars of the board-walk, the water seemed further away than it had the night before. I had only the vaguest idea of how tides worked, other than sometimes they were in and sometimes they were out, and no real desire to learn more, but I realized that it was going to make finding the location of the body harder than I'd antici-pated. Sand pretty much looked like every other bit of sand, without landmarks. And scent was of no use whatsoever, with the brine of salt and fish laying over everything like... well, like the smell of fish. Not the mouth-watering kind, either.

I took a sip from my own thermos, courtesy of the cottage's kitchen, and squinted out over the mottled grey sand, backing up a little to get a wider view. I'd gone at an angle, from here...

'Scuse, miss."

I'd almost bumped into the mangy old tom, too focused on what was in front of me to notice that there was someone behind me. I shook myself back to alertness, aware that that kind of thing could have gotten me shivved in some parts of the Alley — and maybe some parts here, too.

"Sorry, old paws," I said, then did a probably comedic double take. "What are you'd doing?"

He squinted at me, sparse whiskers twitching, then seemed to decide I wasn't actually mocking him. "Beach combing."

The thing in his hands looked more like a mini-vacuum than a comb, but weirder things have been named worse.

He must've seen my confusion, because he let the mini-whatever rest on the sand, leaning on the handle, and explained. "People drop things from there," and he pointed up at the boardwalk, "and they leave 'em on their blankets when they close up shop for the day, and it all falls into the sand, never to be seen again. Some of it, valuable. Coins, jewelry, that sort of thing." He patted the handle fondly. "This baby tells me where they are, so I can dig 'em up. Anything valuable, I can sell."

I nodded. Like dumpster-diving, but less likely to stain your clothing.

"And then there's stuff you can find further down," he went on. "Stuff washes up regular-like, after storms."

My ears flipped forward, and I cursed, trying to play it off as idle curiosity. "Stuff? What, like seaweed? Dead fish?"

"Well, the goal's doubloons — Spanish coin — and whatnot. The harbor here used to be popular with some sailors of less than legal repute, back in the day, and any number of their ships went down, never to be recovered."

I tried not to grin. "Pirates? Here?"

"Free traders," the old tom corrected me, but there was a spark in his eyes that hadn't been there before, so I wasn't certain if he was leading me on or not.

"Once a time was, you could look out over the cliffs just south of here, and see gun battles offshore. And maybe have strangers in your cellar, just passing through on their way to an inlet creek, in heavy-laden canoes."

He shook his head, claws scraping the sparse fur on his chest. "Once a time was. We're far more boring now. Truth is, most of the wrecks were scoured long ago, when they got the tech to do that. Not much more on this beach nowadays than a handful of pocket change and the occasional watch. But it keeps an old puss busy and away from too much daytime T.V."

I laughed politely. "Sounds like a good way to pass an afternoon. I don't suppose you can rent one of those toys?"

"You can rent anything, miss, iffn' you're willing to leave plastic down. There's a pawnshop about a mile down the road, they've got some there. Not as pretty as this one, but if you get the bug, you'll want to buy your own, anyway."

"Thanks. I may give that a try."

He nodded, and we parted ways, him waving the flat end of his combing device over the sand and tilting his head to listen to the faint pings it let off.

I suspected he'd have better hunting than I would. But the idea, once caught on a claw, wouldn't let go.

THE PAWNSHOP WANTED way too damn much to rent — sorry, *redeem* — one of their metal detectors, but I finally haggled them down to something that seemed legal. They even threw in a quick lesson on how to use it, which was appreciated.

I grabbed lunch at a take-out place and was back on the beach by mid-day. The family was long gone, as were the surfers, and for a while at least, I had this stretch of beach to myself. Well, me and the gulls, anyway. Massive, noisy bastards. We eyed each other suspiciously, but I didn't run at them, and they didn't dive at me, so that was good enough for a truce.

The detector was bulkier than I'd imagined, watching the old tom maneuver it, and it took me a while to figure out how to sweep the sand, rather than letting the weight of it pull me forward. But soon enough I had it down, cross-crossing the area where I was pretty sure the body had been.

What did I expect to find? Nothing, if we're going to be honest. Didn't expect anything about this to pan out. But the sky was still blue, I'd gotten used to the smell, and it beat the hell out of sitting in the cottage counting hours until I could go home.

An hour or so in, I'd picked up about a buck thirty in spare change, a lot of beer bottle tops, and incredibly sore forearms, when I heard another ping. I almost ignored it, not really needing the quarter or bottle top, but there's this annoying core of professionalism I'm stuck with that doesn't let me off that easy. So I put the machine down, and started scraping the sand away.

It wasn't a quarter, although it looked like one, size and shape-wise. The metal was different, lighter, and the markings were all wrong.

It also looked like it hadn't been there very long.

"Huh." I flipped the coin between my claws, looking across the sand, back toward the boardwalk, and the arcades. It was probably nothing. But it was a bit more of nothing than I'd had before.

I returned the metal detector to the pawnshop, and got most of my deposit back, then headed back to the boardwalk. The sky had clouded up as the sun dropped, and the few frolickers who'd braved the beach had fled for warmer indoor pursuits. The token in my pocket, I strolled along the boardwalk, heading past the light-up bars toward the darker section.

In warmer weather, these booths would be open, bright lights and noises luring people to waste their cash to win a trashy prize. It was probably a lot of fun, or at least a good distraction. But in the winter, most of the fronts were boarded up, the entire length silent and deserted. I could hear my own steps echoing in the evening air, and if I wasn't accustomed to a similar effect in one of the Alley's less populated corners, I might have been unnerved.

The booth I was looking for was off to the side a bit, the garishly-painted facade mimicking an Old West street front, with "Shoot 'em Up!" across the top in the same script as on the token, the lettering glittering slightly. Under direct light, the colors were probably headache-inducing.

The booth, like all the others, was closed for the season. Anyone who'd dropped the token on the beach recently had either been carrying it around for a while — or had been here recently.

I waited for a minute before approaching, to make sure that nobody else was lurking. The shadows remained empty.

Unlike most of the other booths, which seemed to be open-fronted shacks where would-be competitors lined up outside to play, this one had an actual door, with an actual lock of surprising quality on it. Even without the token, and the dubious connection to the missing presumed dead body, that would have caught my attention. I'm a naturally curious puss like that.

"What do you have in there that's so valuable?"

The lock gave up after only a few minutes, the door swinging open inward without a creak. Hinges oiled and properly aligned. Also interesting.

I let the door swing nearly-shut, then jammed the token into the doorframe, so it couldn't click shut behind me. I paused, waiting to see if anything — anyone — reacted to my arrival.

Nothing. No sound of breathing, no smell of anything other than metal and dust.

Without the reflected lights from town, it was dark enough inside that even my eyes couldn't quite adjust. Fortunately, I'm a smart puss who doesn't go anywhere unprepared, and the narrow beam of the micro flashlight was enough to give me a pretty good idea of what's inside.

"Okay, I can see why you're locked up," I said softly, flicking the beam from one dark figure to another. The inside carried out the mural from outside, set up like an Old West street, complete with swinging saloon doors and hitching posts, and the 'towns-folk' lined up to watch the action. Five sets of footprints were painted onto the floor near where I stood, and at the far end of the booth, my light caught a figure, still and, unlike the other figures, posed to be decidedly menacing. If I hadn't already known there was nothing breathing inside, it might have given me a jolt.

I gathered from the set-up that the trick here was to face off against an animatronic gunslinger. The five sets of footprints were where people would line up — competing against each other, as well as the 'gunslinger?' Probably.

I supposed that it was the kind of thing that would probably appeal to someone who'd never actually faced a gun or a knife, never been in actual danger. My lip curled a little in scorn, even as I felt a faint urge to try my own reflexes against it.

"Not the time," I reminded myself, letting the beam play against the walls, trying to see what was making my whiskers twitch. There were hooks along the long wall where, I presumed, prizes were hung during the season, taunting guests with what they could win, if they only pumped enough money into the game. But something about that wall...

It was too short, I realized suddenly. The 'street' was far narrower than the outside building suggested. So there had to be something on the other side of that wall.

At this point, the missing dead body was pretty much out of my mind. I'm not proud of the fact, but like I said, I'm a curious puss, and this was a curiosity and a puzzle and a place I wasn't supposed to be, all at once. Show me a puss who can resist that, and I'll show you a rabbit in a cat suit.

I hadn't seen a door on the other side of the building. That didn't mean there wasn't one, but generally speaking, you don't hide external doors; you want people to be able to find them. Internal doors, on the other hand...

I let the beam drop, playing it along the floor. Scuffed and dusty, there wasn't anything to see until — huh. Nearly at the corner, the faintest indentation that suggested something was dragged along it, in a half-circle.

The best hidden doors are pocket doors — they don't show drag — but they're also more expensive, built into the wall itself. Folk who want to hide something, but don't want to spend a lot of money — or have outside contractors come in — usually just install a panel door.

The problem with skimping is folk like me. The lock was better on this door, an inset job that required some concentration, the mini-light held in my jaw so I could see what I was manipulating, but it wasn't *that* good, and I had it open easily enough.

In a perfectly innocent world, this space would have been filled with the missing stuffed animals or whatever they give away, or whatever fake pistols they use, or... I had no idea what else might be stored, off-season, honestly.

Instead, the mini-light reflected off sterile-looking white walls and bounced off a long steel table covered with white plastic tubs, tubing, and a series of gas burners, thankfully turned off.

I blinked, and drew in a deep breath that left me coughing in reaction.

I'd stumbled into a nepetalactone lab.

I backed away a little, rubbing at my nose to get the smell out of it, and leaned against the wall, trying to think.

Now, it's not that I have anything against a little 'nip. And it's not exactly a crime to have or use it, no matter how stupidly addictive it can be. But Petal's something else entirely. That's more than 'nip — it's a distilled, incredibly powerful concoction that can override a puss' common sense, and even their basic sense of self-preservation. I'd read and seen enough — a puss on Petal is a puss prone to acts of amazing stupidity that too often leads to death. Either theirs, or someone else'.

It's also nearly impossible to identify as Petal, rather than plain 'nip, until it's too late. Because of all that, it's *not* available on the open market like the leaf version.

And that, naturally, makes it incredibly lucrative.

Which meant that this lab hadn't been left unattended. I

clicked off the light — too late, but better too late than perpetually stupid — and tried to remember if I'd seen any cameras, either outside or in.

No. I mean, I hadn't been looking, but that's the kind of thing that becomes third-nature, after a few years in the PI biz. But I'd been acting under the assumption that this was, probably, an accidental or maybe random death in a hick town, not...

I forced my heart to slow down, dragging a deep breath in and exhaling, quiet as I could. The fact that I'd found the token where the body had been wasn't proof of anything. But it was a damning coincidence I couldn't ignore.

I needed to get the hell out of here, now.

The hidden door slid shut easily, the lock clicking back into place without me having to do anything. Smart criminals, making sure carelessness didn't fuck them up, but good for me too, right now. I tried to remember if I'd touched or moved anything in the main space, decided that no, I hadn't, and backed carefully toward the door, trying to disturb as little of the dust as possible. Reaching up to pull the now-dented token out of the jamb, I slid out the door like a greased ferret, praying nobody was coming around the corner at exactly the wrong moment.

The door snicker shut behind me, and I reset that lock, then straightened, exhaling in relief as nobody yelled at me in alarm. But better not linger, just in case they'd set a silent alarm. I turned, pocketing the token, and let out a tail-fluffing yelp as I ran directly into am incredibly broad — and hard — chest.

"Get on my back."

"What?"

"Get. On. My. Back." The massive head that'd dropped

down to glare at me was easily the size of my entire body, the eyelashes as long as my whiskers. I'd never been that close to a horse before — scratch that, I'd never been close to a horse before, period — but I was pretty sure this was a damned big one. His legs were folded underneath him, which was why I'd run into him in the first place, and I was about to ask him what the hell he was doing when one of his massive ears flicked backward at the same time mine did: someone was coming.

"Get on my back," the horse hissed again, and this time I did, leaping as gently as I could and taking a clawful of coarse mane to hold onto, rather than risk digging into flesh accidentally.

"Ups we go," he said, and suddenly everything below me heaved forward, then back, and suddenly I was human-high from the ground and moving at a slightly terrifying speed down the boardwalk, the clip-clop of hooves echoing off the closed-up shacks.

After a missed heartbeat or two, I realized that the horse was only walking, and the side-to-side motion wasn't all that hard to adjust to, so long as I stayed close to the neck and didn't look down. Or up. Or ahead. Or close my eyes, as I discovered that made things far worse.

But having nothing to do but hang on left my brain too much time to work. Why had I agreed to this? I could have slipped away in the shadows. A horse trotting down the boardwalk seemed the most... non-sneaky exit from a break-in I'd ever imagined.

Nothing seemed to be following us, though. Either the noise we'd heard had no interest in the lab, or horses were a common enough sight here to go unremarked.

"How — "

"Shhhh," the voice came back to me. "Almost there."

I didn't bother asking almost where: I was pretty sure I wouldn't get an answer.

We clopped off the boardwalk and onto a paved road that dead-ended in what looked like an abandoned warehouse. My — companion? Ride? — shouldered aside a half-open sliding door at the side, and something closed it behind us.

I tensed, but then a light flickered on, and I realized that we'd entered not a warehouse, but a barn of some kind. There was a wide alley, and stalls on either side, three to a side, ending in what looked like an enclosed arena.

"Who's the hitchhiker, Chugger?"

"Don't know," my ride — Chugger? — said, moving over to the door of one of the stalls, hooves now muffled on softer flooring. He brushed against the door, and I took the invitation, unhooking my claws from the mane as best I could and leapt to the much more reassuringly solid and still wooden frame.

There was another horse looking back at me, and a small, wire-haired dog weaving in and out of its legs, clearly not worried about getting kicked.

"Found him slipping out of the front, was going to question him but we were about to get interrupted."

"So you brought him here?"

"Hey," I said, sharply. "Not a he, first of all."

"Oh." The second horse looked at me, brown eyes considering. "Sorry."

"Second of all, what the fuck?"

All right, maybe not company language. But it had been a rough day so far.

"We'll be the ones asking questions, miss," Chugger said, and only now, able to see him at eye level, was I able to see how massive he was. Compared to his bulk, the other horse was built like a greyhound. One kick with a hoof, and I'd be Duchess-splatter against the wall.

So, maybe time to be polite, at least until I got a clue what was going on. So far, I was pretty sure they weren't the owners — or clients — of the lab...

"What were you doing in there?"

"In where?" I decided I'd be polite, not that I'd be co-operative.

"I really don't have time or patience for this. What were you doing, poking your whiskers in there, city girl?"

I was going to object to the nickname, then paused and let the facts tumble in my grey matter, coming up with one polished nugget: Chugger, or his stablemate, knew who I was. Or at least, what I'd been doing. Which meant they were either associated with Buster — his bosses, or fellow goons — or...

"Fuck me sideways," I said, sinking down onto my haunches. "You're cops, aren't you."

Retired, it turned out. But apparently while you can take the saddle off a police horse, you can't get 'em out from under the saddle in their own brains.

"We'd been watching them for months," the other horse — Sonny — was saying now. "Seriously, almost a year. The Brock boys bought up the lease, rebuilt the game so it was on an indoor slot. That was enough to make us suspicious, but everything'd been on the legal."

"Except Brock boys don't do legal," Chugger said. "We were pretty sure that something larger was going on. Or about to come down."

"And then they turfed us."

"Mandatory retirement age. Buncha agist crap."

"But we knew we were onto something."

"And we were right." The dog, who'd been quiet until now, had a deeper voice than I'd been expecting from the pipsqueak body. "Two months ago, they shut down for the season, and while they were pulling out the movables for winter storage, they were loading stuff in, too. All the bustle, nobody wound've noticed, except we were watching."

"Oh, that's Whitey," Chugger said, as though suddenly remembering the dog was there. "Our squeal."

"I prefer confidential informant," the dog said.

"Yeah, whatever. But he was right. Two months ago, they load the equipment in, and we've got two humans slipping in at odds hours. But no reason to go in, and without a reason and a warrant, anything we found wouldn't be admissible."

Never mind the fact that they were retired now. I didn't bother pointing that out.

"So now you know who we are what's your story?"

"Name's Duchess. I'm a private investigator. And I'm not on a job," I added before they could get the wrong idea. "Seriously, I was just supposed to be here for a long weekend while things cleared up back home."

"You're from the Alley, yeah, we figured that."

I switched an ear at Sonny, who gave a horsy snort, which came with a full-on gust of musty breath. "I did my time on pavement, puss. I know city cats when I see 'em."

Fair enough.

"So, little miss long weekend ends up just happening to poke her whiskers into a boarded-up game shack that also just happens to be a suspected petal den?"

"Weirdly, enough, yeah?" I thought about it for a second, then decided to go for broke. It's not like I had much to lose, and they're retired, anyway. Nothing that happened here was official or on the books.

"It started with a kid knocking on my door..."

By the time I got through, Sonny had trotted off to get me some water, and I wetted my whiskers while they put their muzzles together and muttered at each other. The squeal,

Whitey, sat next to the fence I was squatting on, and studied me thoughtfully.

"What?"

"What's it like? They Alley?"

Save me from small-town scammers who think the big city's the answer to all their low-life dreams. Like we don't have enough home-grown already?

"Cold and nasty and crowded," I told him. "Trust me, you've got more chances here."

He might've argued with me, or maybe not, but the horses came to some kind of conclusion, and both heads swung back to look at me. I figured they were going to ask for more details on the lab itself, maybe ask me to sneak back in, and I was about to preemptively excuse myself from whatever they had planned, when they changed the game.

"The body. We think we know who it was."

Turned out they'd had a potential squeal, a low-level runner for the Brock brothers who'd been fetching and delivering for the lab for a few weeks. Sonny had been working on him for months before then, and they'd really thought this would be the break they'd needed, to get enough details back to the station house and get an official file opened.

And then the runner had disappeared. The day before the kit found his flotsam in the sand.

"I'd just gotten him softened up, too," Sonny said. "That's the risk, though; the moment they start to have doubts, or get greedy for a second payout, it's like their bosses can sniff it on 'em. And then they end up snoot-down in the sand."

He seemed more upset about the loss of info than the fact that he'd gotten his snitch killed. I supposed it went with the obsession. I'd seen it before with lifers; they lose track of the small wins and think only the big ones count.

Not my problem, though. I'd found the answer to the kid's

question: who the body was, and how they died, and there wasn't anything I could do about it.

"So, his people killed him and... what, dumped him as a warning?" It made sense, I supposed. If this was the winter moneymaker, when the summer tourist money dried up, the money-*takers* in town would want to make sure nothing else disturbed it. And sending Buster after me — I guess they thought a wink and a claw would be enough to get me to back off, since I wasn't the one the warning had been for...

"But the body wasn't actually found by anyone except a teenager, and then it disappeared. You don't get much mileage out of that. If bodies actually wash up on a regular basis, I'd think they'd have picked..."

The horses exchanged sideways glances, which was weird to see, since their eyes literally were on the sides of their head, and it clicked for me.

"You needed actual evidence because you think they've got someone at the station. You think the message was meant for a dirty cop, warning them to keep their jaws shut. And you think they found it and dragged it away so no questions would be raised." Or connected back to them. Which in turn would tie them more tightly to our drug-runners, if they'd covered up a killing.

That was a leap of logic, even for me, but damned if it didn't make all the loose bits shake into place.

"It's... a theory," Chugger admitted. "Short of seagulls making off with the body in under an hour, which is unlikely and more than a little horrifying to consider — "

All three of the locals gave a full-body shudder at that. Thinking of some of the birds I'd seen, their hooked beaks larger than my entire paw, I felt a shudder in my own spine as well. Rats were one thing; winged rats were another entirely.

"The Brock brothers have always kept their noses clean, officially. Considering how many dead ends have *almost* led to them... yeah, we think maybe someone in the department's gone dirty. But whoever they are, they're good at the paperwork. If we can clean this up without burning them, maybe they can be useful."

Not gonna lie, it's weirdly reassuring to discover that small town cops are, if anything, even more cynical than Alley woofers.

But as much fun as all this had been, my part in it was done, and I had no interest in getting dragged into post-departmental cookouts. "All right then," I said, stretching my hind legs a little, preparing to jump down to the ground. "I'm glad I could be helpful, and thanks for the exit route, but this sounds like it's a local issue, and..."

"We need your help."

"No, you really don't."

"We can't get into the lab."

"Because you're retired cops?"

"Because we're too damn big."

Oh. Right. That would be an issue.

"I've already told you what I saw."

"A lab itself isn't enough. At most, after some legal bargaining it goes down as a misdemeanor, assuming we could even pin it to them. Which we can't, not now. But they killed the runner. And if a cop covered that up..."

"You could break open the entire thing, and clean house." And it would have to be them, because odds were, nobody still on the job was going to risk their job, if this went deeper than one dirty officer. They already had their pensions; they were effectively untouchable.

But they needed evidence. And the squeal, as eager as he might be, probably wasn't a reputable witness they could use to request a warrant. Me, idiot walking into this entire mess, with my license and my reputation? Yeah, I'd do just fine.

I sighed. Maybe Sparks was right, and I was just doomed to find trouble no matter where I went. "What do you need me to do."

---

BY THE TIME we got back to the boardwalk, whoever'd startled us originally had come and gone, but a group of teenagers had set up camp, noisily drinking and carousing around and over the closed-up sheds. I figured we were going to have to put it off, or wait for them to get drunk enough to fall asleep, but Sonny trotted right up to them like the four hoofbeats of doom.

"Awwwww, come on', Cap."

Clearly, they knew him. And had no fear of him, despite their objections, from the way some of them dashed around his hooves, playing tag under his belly without fear,

"Nope. Joey, mind your brother. Souzie, that had better not be a joint I'm smelling. Come on, all of you, you know we've got a curfew so everyone underage skedaddle home, and the rest of you, pack up and take this to the beach where I assume you have a permit?"

There were grumbles and groans, but they started packing up. Sonny watched them with his ears pricked forward, the lamps overhead casting a massive shadow across the weathered boards.

"He was community affairs officer for a bunch of years," Chugger said, a chuckle in his tone. "Knows every damn kid in the neighborhood, and all their bigger brothers and sisters too, still."

"We've got a few coppers like that too," I said. "Nothing official, they just..." I let my voice trail off. It'd been years, but I still missed Dickie. I knew Sparks did, too, even if we were both too tough to ever admit it.

"Okay, we're up," Chugger said, reacting to some sign I'd totally missed. "Come on."

The boys did a once-over around the building, then waved me in like I was a rookie on first patrol. I sniffed and finished grooming a paw before sauntering my way under the streetlamp and disappeared into the shadows at the edge of the building. Like I needed someone to tell me the way was clear, but I could hear Sparks' voice in my ear, reminding me that I was the guest and the volunteer here, and needed to play nice. Or polite, at least.

"I'm always polite," I told the silent judgement, and could practically hear his snort in response, never mind he was miles away probably up to his tail in paperwork, right now.

Sucked to be him.

I went in the same way I'd gotten in before; if anyone had checked the door, they hadn't put a new, more difficult lock on it. Probably they hadn't even noticed it had been picked; I'd done the job right.

The main room looked the same, but the figures were a little creepier than before, now that I knew what was on the other side — and the thought that someone might have been killed here. The floor was too dark and the lights too dim to show blood, but I'm not ashamed to admit I didn't stay and sniff around.

The moment I slipped into the lab, though, I knew that someone had been there. Things had been moved. I couldn't point to any one thing and say, "this wasn't where it had been," but the sense of the room was different, and I could feel my fur fluffing, an instinctive reaction trying to make myself more threatening to anything still lurking.

But whoever had been there was long gone.

But because they'd gone didn't mean they might not come back and bring reinforcements. I might be able to sneak away in the shadows, but the two waiting outside couldn't, and never mind they were locals with reason to be on the boardwalk, it wouldn't do any good for any of us for them to be eyeballed.

And if the Brock bothers thought the lab had been compromised, they'd shut it down in a minute flat. Which was no skin off my paw, but I found myself rooting for the hoof brigade, at this point. They'd worked hard for a win.

I did a once-over of the space, just noting the things that felt different, not touching anything, just looking. All the years of training myself to identify details, to catch the shadow of something that didn't fit the rest of the scene, and my eye was drawn back to the table.

The notebook. It might have been on the table before, but it had been closed. Now, it was open, the two narrow-lined pages visible filled with notations and formulas in several different colors, but what looked like the same hand, short, firm strokes made with confidence, and maybe a little bit of a distracted rush.

Wild guess, but a logbook of formulas in a Petal lab might be useful as evidence. Statement of intent, at the very least, and the defense of 'this was dropped into my hands by an unknown benefactor' had held up under worse circumstances...

Not that I'd ever had anything to do with that.

My ears twitch at the muffled sound of *something* happening on the other side of the wooden walls, and before I second-guessed myself, I snatched the notebook up and skedaddled.

In the minute, maybe three it took for me to check and relock the doors behind me, the sounds had stopped, and never mind that the shapes were wrong, the silhouette is all-too-familiar to me: two cops, standing over a downed perp.

Standing *on* the perp, it looked like. Although I'm pretty sure Sonny's wasn't putting any weight on that hoof. The threat of it's enough to keep the human down.

Try that in the Alley, and... I'm not sure what would happen, actually. Humans don't come down there often, and when they do, they're tough enough to hold their own.

"Hey," I called, and even as Sonny turned to look, the human proved me wrong about the threat, shoving and wriggling hard enough to throw the hoof off his chest, scrambled to his feet and disappeared into the shadows like he's got ferret in his DNA.

"Damn," Chugger cursed, and started to go after him, then sighs. "He was dumb enough to get caught, but I don't think he's dumb enough to admit it to anyone."

"Might just've been looking for a place to sleep," Sonny says. "I didn't recognize the face."

"They all look alike anyway," Chugger said. "What've you got there, city girl?"

I'd almost forgotten the notebook. I held it up, letting it drop open to the last page that had been written in, the lamplight enough just to see the shapes of the ink.

"Whoever was in there earlier, they'd opened this, and left it on the table, like they were adding or checking something, so I figured..."

If I'd gone in prepared, I'd have had a camera to get pictures of it, and not had to take the whole thing, which was a dead giveaway that someone had been there, but I hadn't and I wasn't and I hadn't, and there was no point in bringing any of that up now.

"Better hope it's something good," Sonny said. "Because something like that goes missing, they're gonna notice."

And no point bringing it up because they were thinking the same thing I was. Worse now, because if the human had been connected, and he tried to shift the blame for the missing note-book, he had a description to give them.

"Whitey can tell us what it says. Come on," and Chugger dropped his neck low enough that I could reach his mane. "Hop on, we're going to have to run."

Oh, yay.

<hr>

IF SOMEONE WERE to offer me a deal that I'd never have to get on a horse's back again ever, in exchange for one of my lives, I'd probably take it. I prefer to do my running-away low to the ground, not clinging to a strip of leather with all twenty claws while a couple-hundred pounds of horse pounded pavement below me at thirty miles an hour faster than should be legal.

Not to mention, even on the boardwalk, horses are not what anyone would call inconspicuous. Not that I could tell if anyone was watching, because I'm not ashamed to admit that my face was buried in Chugger's mane the entire time, mainly so I didn't have to see how fast we were moving past things.

If the Maker'd intended us to go that fast, we would've been born with wings.

"You can let go now."

"Easy for you to say." I wasn't sure my claws *could* unclench, at that point; the muscles in my pads had tightened so hard, it *hurt* to retract them. But never let it be said a little pain ever kept me from doing the thing —

After which I promptly lost what was left of my balance, and fell off, twisting mid-way down so that I landed on my feet, and not my dignity.

The squeal — Whitey — dashed forward and grabbed the notebook without so much as a please or thank you. Not that I'd expected a squeal to have manners, but still.

"Can you make paws or tails of it?" I asked, flexing my own paws carefully, trying to work some feeling back into the pads.

"Give me minute" he said, irritated the way only tiny dogs ever get. His ear flopped over and he shook his head to get it to flip back, turning pages fast enough I had my doubts he was actually reading anything, but then, I like to take my time with words, roll around in them a little.

But Whitey didn't look like he was rolling around in anything pleasant. His short-muzzled face started to look pinched, and his black-lined lip pulled back like he was going to snarl, though no sound came out.

"Well?" Chugger pawed a little at the flooring, and that got his vocal cords moving again.

"This ain't good."

I always hate hearing that.

"So, okay, this is a basic formula, pretty much standard here," and one paw tapped the top of the left-hand page. "But then... It's not Petal. Or, it is Petal, but it's not. Not really. They've fucked up the chemistry. Intentionally fucked it up. Counterfeit Petal. You take the base ingredients, and — "

"Don't need to pass an exam, Whitey, don't need the details right now. What's not good about that, and how not-good is it?"

I hadn't known horses could sound menacing; it must be something they teach 'em at the Academy.

"Counterfeit Petal's cheaper to make. The base is what's expensive, and then you cut it with cheaper shit, charge the same amount, there's still enough to fuck someone up for a night, and the profit margin's maybe two, three times. Mostly it's... you just get a weaker product, and eventually word comes down that your product's sub-par, you start losing sales, it's a death spiral and bad for business."

"That's not what they did?" Chugger wouldn't look so

worried if they were in the process of putting themselves out of business.

"No. This, the formula they're using... it's just as potent. Only a hell of a lot deadlier. Like, I'd guess maybe a third of their clients are going to start bleeding into their grey matter, the third or fourth time they snort this stuff."

It would have been nice to say that we were shocked, shocked that drug dealers would kill off their clientele, but the most that got was a wet snort of disgust from Sonny. Higher profits trumped any lingering moral qualms for a particular class of business folk, and there was always going to be another wave of idiots looking for a cheap high and not worrying particularly about the quality.

I'm good at helping people; I don't pretend I'm gonna save 'em. And some folk you just can't save from themselves.

"We need to shut this down," Whitey said.

"Well, yeah. But how? We're still sitting on evidence we can't put into the record," Sonny knocked a hoof toward the ledger, still under the squeal's paws, and snorted in disgust, "and while pretty puss over there is probably a reputable witness, getting her under oath opens a whole new barrel of weevils."

Because I'd stolen the ledger, no two ways around it. Well, there were actually three or four ways around it, but I'd have problems with one or two and I suspected my hooved companions would have issues with all of them.

The squeal didn't look like he'd have a problem with any of them, though, from the eye-rolling he was doing.

"Look, I'm all for making money while money's to be made," he said. "But a dog's gotta have a line. And this," and his paw patted the page gently, "this is pretty much it for me. You do something and people die, hey it happens. You do something and you *know* people are gonna die, and you don't give 'em at least a heads-up? I didn't see any warning labels on the baggies they're distributing, did you?"

I hadn't seen any baggies at all but kept that to myself.

"So, what're you suggesting, Whitey?"

"I bag the ledger. Everyone knows my skill set, yeah? I say they brought me in for a job interview, I didn't like the hang of their jowls, said no, scrammed with the ledger when they weren't looking. Sat on it for a while, then decided you toose could be trusted with something this hot and not burn me, too."

As plans went, it wasn't horrible, actually. I didn't know this copshop, but if I'd brought that story to Captain Sparks, with a known CI willing to perjure themselves for it, he probably would've taken it up the chain.

It all depended on if the ponies were willing to play.

That took another fifteen minutes of muzzle-to-muzzle argument, which the squeal and I were explicitly excluded from. I didn't take offense. That shit was above my pay grade even if I was getting paid for this, which, I reminded myself, I was not.

"So." Whitey looked at me consideringly. "What's it like, the Alley?"

"Like anywhere. Just more expensive." I hoped to hell he wasn't going to ask me for a letter of introduction or anything else idiotic. The Alley might not eat him up in his first week, but even the best small-town grifters took damage when they tried to play in the bigger leagues, and he seemed like a decent enough woofer, for his size.

"Okay." Chugger came over, his long face and rheumy brown eyes looking even more doleful. Was there ever such a thing as a happy horse? I wasn't sure I wanted to see what that looked like, honestly. "This is how it's going to go down. Whitey, you and Sonny are going to take the ledger to the station. You're not going to talk to anybody and I mean anybody until Sonny tells you to sing, you clear on that? And then you only say what he tells you to say."

"You don't trust me to lie convincingly?"

"You feck this up and it's my pension that goes into the drains, so no."

Whitey rolled his eyes again. "Fair enough."

"And you're coming with me," Chugger went on, turning to look at me.

"Wait, what?"

"You don't want to see this all the way through?"

"Not particularly, no." I wanted to go back to my little cottage to try to take a nap, maybe read a trashy novel, drink a beer, wait out the rest of my tenure here until I could go home without anyone else asking me to do anything. I'd made a stupid promise to a kid and I'd fulfilled it, much to my own surprise. I should have been free and clear now, and I was about to say so when Chugger dropped his head down to face level, so close I could smell the grain on his breath.

"You and I, we're going to go track down someone who might know something worth us knowing. And I may need someone with your particular skills to help get it out of them."

If someone'd said that to me in the Alley, I would have made my excuses and backed the hell out of there, double-time. Unless they were compensating me generously, anyway, and maybe not even then. I'm not a bruiser, nor do I play one on the silver screen. But Chugger was a cop — retired or not — and I was reasonably sure, based on our admittedly brief acquaintance, that he wasn't going to ask me to shred someone's face.

Reasonably sure.

"And if I say no?"

"Then when I fill out the inevitably endless paperwork turning this little escapade into something official, I will have no choice but to bring your name into it, prominently, as the concerned citizen who connected the dots for us — all totally you being a hero, of course. You stumbled across badness and realized it was bad stuff, and came to us like a good little squeal..."

The hiss that escaped me at that was involuntary, but I didn't bother to apologize to Whitey. He knew what he was and so did everyone else in the barn.

"And, of course, that would require me to come down and give a statement or seven, and possibly be called to testify if this ever made it to court." Chugger was right in that I knew how to connect dots. Especially when they combined to make an ever-so-subtle threat.

"It is entirely possible," Chugger allowed, his tail swishing slowly. I resisted the urge to swipe at it; that would have been petty, and at this angle I probably would have missed, anyway.

"Fine. And thank you for confirming my opinion of cops, retired or otherwise. You all suck."

---

HE MAY'VE SUCKED, but I'd give Chugger this: he sucked efficiently. Or, more likely, he'd been holding this particular individual in his back pocket until he had questions he already knew the answer to, to ask.

That's how you gauged a squeal's veracity: ask 'em shit you already knew, that they didn't know you knew, and move your way into the answers you *didn't* know. Or so I've been told by those who do this on a semi-professional level.

I preferred cash and favors, myself. A good source didn't need used once and thrown away, it should be used over and over again until it ran dry. But cash, for cops, equaled bribery, and they frowned on that, officially.

Anyway, we didn't waste time actually hunting for his

target, but trotted on up to his doorstep. Literally. He lived in a little cottage not that far from where I'd been staying, but in a different neighborhood entirely. The kind that had La-Z-Boys out on the porch, and grass growing high enough to hide bodies decomposing, if you were willing to overlook the smell, and pretty much everyone was.

He had some pretty flowers growing along the porch, though; some kind of tiny roses that made my nose twitch happily. I saw Chugger's ear twitch toward them and dug my claws lightly into his neck. "Don't eat the flowers," I hissed. "Not unless you *want* to piss him off straightaway."

"Not a rookie," Chugger muttered back, but turned his head to look at the door, instead. "Go ring the doorbell, will ya?"

By the time I'd gotten onto the porch, though, the door was already opening, and a brindle tabby was staring me square in the eye.

So that was why Chugger'd wanted me along. Nobody can read a puss like another puss.

"Whatchoowant?" Then his gaze slipped past me to where Chugger waited, and I could see the decision flash through his brain: stand, or run?

He decided to stand, closing the door behind him and leaned against it like he didn't have a care in the world, and it was perfectly normal for cops to stop by to shoot the breeze on any random afternoon.

Hell, maybe it was. I'd only been in town a few days, and I wouldn't be surprised.

"Hello, Begley."

"Officer Chugs."

Chugger didn't remind him that him that he was retired.

"You don't mind if we ask you a few questions, do you?"

"Would objectin' do me any good? Nah, I didn't think so. So, go ahead, but make it quick, I got an overnight sleeping upstairs and I don't wanna have to explain you to her, if you know what I mean."

"Girl's got a right to know what she's getting into," Chugger said, mock-scolding. "Or have you turned over a new leaf? Gone legal an' law-abiding?"

"Maybe I have," Begley said.

"And maybe you haven't." He nodded to me, and I pulled the token out of my pocket, showing it to him. "This look familiar? I seem to remember you having one on you, last time you got pulled over."

"Maybe I do, maybe I don't got one. Tokens are junk around here, you know that."

"Junk that gives me cause to believe that you might know something about the hinky business being conducted at the Wild West Shootout booth, down the boardwalk."

"What, a gallery scam? Pffft." He licked a paw and smoothed down the fur over one shoulder. "Too much up-front investment for my taste, you know that."

"You mean, you could never find someone to front you the cash," I said. I didn't know for certain, but the type was standard-issue, and he fit all the stereotypes.

"Look, I don't have a lot of time to spend on you, and my hooves are aching, so let's cut to the chase, all right? The Petal operation. One of their people ended up face down in the sand. You happen to know anything about how that went down? Just hearsay and rumor, naturally."

"Lots of people go face down in the sand around here, Officer Chugs. It's Point Promise."

"Work with me, Begley, and you can go back to snuggling before dinner. Give me grief, and I might have to bring my equine ass into your front parlor, and park it for a while."

Begley cut eyes in my direction, like he was looking for sympathy. I gave it, with a faint shrug and a 'what can you do?'

flick of my ears. "All we want to know is why the mook got offed. Did he dip a claw where he shoudn't've? Hear something not for his ears? Dip wick into someone else's wax pot?"

A twitch of his tail, nearly hidden against the door, caught my eye. I wasn't sure if Chugger had seen it, though, or knew how to read it.

"That was it, wasn't it? He was dipping somewhere he shouldn't have. And the bosses killed him?"

"It wasn't like that." Begley seemed offended I'd assumed sex was involved, from the way his ears went flat.

"No?" Chugger shifted, like he was about to try to climb the porch stairs. Considering they'd barely held under my weight, that was enough of a threat to get Begley talking again.

"He was dipping, but it wasn't his wick. Idiot got hooked on the product."

"And it killed him. Because it's cut with shit."

"It's what?"

"You didn't know? Stuff you're running, they've changed the formula. Quick high, probable death."

Begley's ears went flat again, and his pupils contracted in a way that the shade of the porch couldn't account for. I'm not much of a hunter by inclination, but I could practically feel my whiskers quiver with the need to pounce while he was in shock.

"They killed him, Begley." Chugger's voice had gone from stern to soothing, the kind of voice he probably used when they put neighborhood kids on his back to jog around in a circle at community fairs, to show them how approachable the local cops could be. "They killed him sure as they put a gun to his head. And then they dumped him — "

"We did that." The twitch of the tail had turned into a lashing. "We didn't want them to know he'd been dipping, so we dragged him... figured, by the time the body washed up, they wouldn't be able to tell what did him in, right? Who was going to bother with an autopsy on a floater nobody, waste taxpayer dollars..."

The lashing intensified, slapping against the wood of the door with a dull thud thud thud that could become hypnotic if it didn't stop soon.

"They take good care of their people, if you run into trouble. Bail, or medical, or whatever. Or if you die. But if they found out he'd been dipping, they wouldn't do shit. His sisters were counting on that money, Chugs. We had to do something."

"Yeah, I get it. I do."

"And if I squeal on 'em, nobody gets nothing. I ain't gonna do that."

"We can get you protection, Begley. Get you out of this town, somewhere else."

"And do what? No, sorry, officer Chugs, no can do. Not gonna squeal."

"You got that token on you still?" I suspected he had; most pusses only wear collars and tags on formal occasions, or if they're into that kink, but he had something hanging around his neck, and the fur was matted enough around it to suggest he never took it off. "Because I bet it matches this one here, found on the body of a dead suspect... That's cause enough to bring someone in for questioning, isn't it, officer?"

"If we drag you in unwilling, it makes far more of a splash than you giving us details on the quiet," Chugger said, less-bad cop a good look on him. "A name, Begley. A meeting place. Something. There're always other jobs, but these guys, they're going to keep killing people just because they wanted to feel good. You think that's something to protect?"

The tabby gave a sour twitch of his whiskers. Nobody liked being told, however indirectly, that they have to choose between greed, and knowing their greed let other people die. And if you're not a sociopath or a stone-cold killer, there's really only one way you can jump, after that.

---

"WELL, THAT WAS FUN," I said as we walked back down to the street. A group of teenagers raced toward us, then seemed to realize who they were about to barrel into and veered into the trees to avoid us.

"Look before you run over a car," Chugger shouted at them, and two of the boys gave vaguely unironic salutes as they veered again and headed up the walk and into one of the houses down the block.

"It's not just Sonny who knows every kid in this town, is it?" I shook off his response as we turned the corner and headed back toward my own — temporary — neighborhood. "Like I said, it's been fun, and I hope you close the files on this with a responding slam of jail cells, but I'm out. Really and truly for serious, out. You've got more than enough to go on, and I am not going to come back and testify officially, so just get that thought out of your head now."

I gathered breath to rebut whatever objection he might muster, but nothing came, the sound of hooves and swishing tail the only noise other than the dull roar of engines on another street.

"Yes. You're right. Although once this case becomes official, they would of course compensate you for your travel..."

"Yeah, I've waited on municipal reimbursements before. No thanks." I paced a few yards ahead and turned around to look at Chugger as we walked, a complicated skill, but one I'd found useful over my lives. "So...just like that?"

Horses aren't built to shrug, but I'd swear the bruiser managed it. "Unlike Begley, you're of more potential use to me off the record and still speaking to me than dragged in, unwilling."

I snorted. Now that's the cop attitude I knew and could respect.

<hr>

It took another three days before I got the all-clear from back home. I spent most of it sleeping — there was a spot in the lounge area where the sunlight lingered all afternoon — and ordering in from the local deli. I didn't go near the ocean and didn't miss it at all.

The trip home seemed to take forever, but when the train finally pulled into the station, I grabbed my bag and hopped onto the platform like a sailor hitting soil after six months on the worst seas, a little wobbly, but glad enough to kiss the planking.

"Welcome home."

And, like the sailor, I had a welcoming committee, although thankfully Sparks did not try to kiss me.

"Please tell me you're not going to tell me I have to leave again," I said, tossing my bag at him. He caught it, tucking the handle into his harness like a good woofer, and turning to walk out with me. "Because I'm not going."

"I know you're not a small-town puss, but was it really that boring?"

"Captain, you have no idea."

# ABOUT THE AUTHOR

Laura Anne Gilman's work has been hailed as "a true American myth" by NPR, and praised for her "deft plotting and first-class characters" by Publishers Weekly. She has won the Endeavor Award for THE COLD EYE, and been shortlisted for a Nebula, (another) Endeavor, and a Washington State Book Award. Her novels include the Locus-bestselling weird western Devil's West trilogy, the Cosa Nostradamus urban fantasy series, and the Vineart War trilogy, and the story collections WEST WINDS' FOOL and DARKLY HUMAN. A former New Yorker, she currently lives outside of Seattle with two cats and many deadlines.

Join Laura Anne's Patreon here: https://www.patreon.com/LAGilman

Sign up for Laura Anne's newsletter here: https://mailchi.mp/2cc5d5547cb1/gilmanquarterly

More information, social media links, and updates can be found at https://www.lauraannegilman.net/

www.ingramcontent.com/pod-product-compliance
Lightning Source LLC
Chambersburg PA
CBHW070308120726